Rocket City, Alabam'

by Mark Saltzman

A PLAY WITH SONGS OF THE AMERICAN SOUTH

A SAMUEL FRENCH ACTING EDITION

SAMUEL FRENCH

FOUNDED 1830

NEW YORK HOLLYWOOD LONDON TORONTO

SAMUELFRENCH.COM

ISBN 978-0-573-69757-9   Printed in U.S.A.   #29199

RENTAL MATERIALS

An orchestration consisting of a **Piano/Conductor Score** will be loaned two months prior to the production ONLY on the receipt of the Licensing Fee quoted for all performances, the rental fee and a refundable deposit.

Please contact Samuel French for perusal of the music materials as well as a performance license application.

IMPORTANT BILLING AND CREDIT
REQUIREMENTS

All producers of *ROCKET CITY, ALABAM'* *must* give credit to the Author of the Play in all programs distributed in connection with performances of the Play, and in all instances in which the title of the Play appears for the purposes of advertising, publicizing or otherwise exploiting the Play and/or a production. The name of the Author *must* appear on a separate line on which no other name appears, immediately following the title and *must* appear in size of type not less than fifty percent of the size of the title type.

ROCKET CITY, ALABAM' was first produced by the Alabama Shakespeare Festival in Montgomery, Alabama as *ROCKET CITY* on April 20, 2008. *ROCKET CITY* was developed in association with the Southern Writers' Project, a program of the Alabama Shakespeare Festival (Geoffrey Sherman, producing artistic director). The performance was directed by David Ellenstein, with sets by Michael Schwiekardt, costumes by Susan Branch, music direction by Brett Rominger, lighting by Mike Post, sound design by Richelle Thompson, and dramaturgy by Susan Willis. The production stage manager was Sara Lee Howell, the production assistant was Kerrie Riber. The cast was as follows:

AMY LUBIN. . . . . Lori Prince

MAJOR HAMILTON PIKE, JR.. . . . . Fletcher McTaggart

JED KESSLER. . . . . Daniel Cameron Talbott

WERNHER VON BRAUN. .Matt Bradford Sullivan

ISRAEL WATKINS . . . . .James Bowen

HARRY S. TRUMAN, BENJY, LEMUEL DECATUR,
      LESTER PRUITT, ROCKET VOICE . . . . Paul Hopper

GENERAL BARKLEE, HEINZ KLAUBER,
      RABBI BENJAMIN, ANNOUNCER . . . . Ralph Elias

SUSANNA PRUITT, SARAH. . . . . Greta Lambert

BERTINA DUPRAY, EUVELLA, BARONESS VON BRAUN . . . . Suzanna Hay

This play was developed in the Hothouse at the Playhouse
program at Pasadena Playhouse.

CHARACTERS

AMY LUBIN – Young New York woman, early 20s

MAJOR HAMILTON PIKE, JR. – American blue-blood, Princeton-educated Army officer. Mid-20s to early 30s

JED KESSLER – Amy's Alabama-born fiancé, 20s

WERNHER VON BRAUN* – The German rocket genius. Mid-30s to early 40s

ISRAEL WATKINS (plays guitar) – Alabama-born, African-American truck driver. 30s to early 40s

CHARACTER MAN 1 – Harry S. Truman, Benjy in London, Lemuel Decatur, Lester Pruitt, Rocket Voice

CHARACTER MAN 2 – General Barklee, Heinz Klauber, Rabbi Benjamin, TV Announcer

CHARACTER WOMAN 1 – Susanna Pruitt, Sarah in London

CHARACTER WOMAN 2 – Bertina Dupray, Euvella, Polly, Baroness Von Braun

*Note: Characters in the play who speak German correctly pronounce Von Braun's name: "VEH-nah fahn BRAH-oon." The R in "Braun" is lightly rolled.

These character roles can be distributed among more actors, if budgets and talent pool permit.

If there isn't a guitar-playing actor available to play Israel Watkins, a guitarist might be added to the cast to accompany Israel when he sings. In that case, the actor playing Israel might play the harmonica, if he has that skill. The overall goal is to have an authentic acoustic delta blues feel to the blues music.

SETTING

This play is set mostly in Huntsville, Alabama in the early 1950's. It's performed by a minimum of nine actors, 6 Male (5 White, one African-American) 3 Female (White).

This story is based on true events.

AUTHOR'S NOTE

The historical facts, the real events, of this play are all readily research-able – e.g. the career of Wernher Von Braun, the development and launch of America's Redstone Missile, the post-war history of Hunstville, Alabama, and the German rocket bombing of London. It is historical truth that Huntsville, to this day, is home to a Jewish community dating back to the 19th century. And like any typical American town during and following WWII, Huntsville had an anti-German mindset. When that attitude thawed, yes, baskets of German food were brought around to welcome the new immigrants.

Some notes on the music: Though *Rocket City, Alabam'* is not a musical, a music director is most likely needed for any production. The character playing Israel Watkins provides the musical element of the show and ideally, an African-American singer-actor-guitarist is cast as Israel. But if your singing-actor can't play guitar, a guitarist, preferably African-American, should be added to the cast. In this case, Israel would be a solo singer (and perhaps harmonica player) with a back-up guitarist. But preferable by far is Israel as a classic Delta bluesman, playing his own acoustic guitar.

Musically, the first act is blues and the second act, gospel and spirituals. (This play, on one level, is about traveling from the Earth to a higher altitude.) The blues songs should never be sung slowly, never in the grim, moaning style of blues, but rather the aggressive, hard-driving blues style. "Alabama Bound" should be performed with railroad propulsion. "Poor Boy" is biting and driving. The gospel songs of Act Two are also up tempo. The music should accelerate the play, never slow it down.

The solo guitar underscoring is loose and improvised. All of the following are valid approaches to the guitar underscoring and can be used alternately: Playing the given melody note for note, improvising on the melody, or just strumming the chords. All are valid approaches to the underscoring which, of course, must always stay in the background, and never compete with the spoken dialogue.

And one note on the set – putting a missile on stage need not be daunting. Really, it's just a big empty cylinder painted with the markings of a Redstone Missile.

–Mark Saltzman

Special thanks to Arnold Mittelman/
American Theater Festival - National Jewish Theater

ACT ONE

Scene One – Harry Speaks

(Late 1940's/early 1950's period music of the pre-rock, bland E-Z listening type: Perry Como, Kate Smith, Patti Page, instrumentals by Liberace or Manitovani. Nothing swingin' or jazzy or "cool." This soothing, gentle music is interrupted by: A HUGE, THUNDERING BOOM! Over the fading sound, **PRESIDENT HARRY S. TRUMAN** *appears in his characteristic suit, bowtie and wire-rim glasses.)*

PRESIDENT TRUMAN. My fellow Americans. This is President Harry S. Truman. The news I have to bring you tonight is not happy news. But we are a strong nation. We've come through a war together and we're going to come through this.

At 1:04 yesterday afternoon, the Soviet Union detonated their first atomic bomb. Yes, we are no longer the only atomic power in the world, but even so, our nation still stands tall with a mighty military that day and night watches our skies and protects us from catastrophe and obliteration. So sleep well.

(back to music)

Scene Two – General Barklee's Office
In The Pentagon

(**MAJOR HAMILTON PIKE JR.** *stands before* **GENERAL BARKLEE.** *Major Pike is about 30, one of the new generation of Cold War warriors. The General, a Southerner of the older generation, still lives in his WWII glory. Major Pike carries a rolled-up map. Just a moment ago, he set a document on the General's desk, awaiting signature.*)

GENERAL. Our country has never been in greater danger. That's what the President said to us at the briefing. He wants to know what we're doing. Or, in his words, what you lame-brain lazy bastards in the Pentagon are doing.

MAJOR PIKE. Sounds like Mr. Truman. General Barklee, it's exactly because of this situation that you must sign this document immediately.

GENERAL. Which is this?

MAJOR PIKE. It will put one of the army arsenals under my command.

GENERAL. I don't sign over something without knowing what's what.

MAJOR PIKE. It's a classified project, sir.

GENERAL. I'm the head of Army ordnance, Major Pike! Classified projects my left buttock. What do you want with my arsenal?

MAJOR PIKE. I thought your signature would be merely a formality, sir.

GENERAL. Major, you'll answer my question.

(**PIKE** *realizes this won't be an easy sell and slows down, as if speaking to a child.*)

MAJOR PIKE. Yes, sir, General Barklee. Weapons development. The Russians now have the A-bomb. And we have the A-bomb. But we have no way of delivering it.

GENERAL. You got a bomb, you drop it from a plane! Good enough in the last war, wasn't it?

MAJOR PIKE. That war is over, sir. The Russians have their anti-aircraft guns, we have ours. A plane carrying an A-bomb would be detected and shot down miles from its target. The delivery system will now be guided missiles, and we need a place to build them. So if you'll just sign this…

GENERAL. *(reminding* **PIKE** *of his rank)* Which army arsenal are you REQUESTING that I authorize?

MAJOR PIKE. I have a map right here. Let me show you.

(The **MAJOR** *unrolls his map and looks for a place to hang it.)*

MAJOR PIKE. This won't quite work…

GENERAL. Put it on the other wall or something.

MAJOR PIKE. Not enough room. I'll just spread it out here…

*(***PIKE** *rolls out the map on the floor and gets to his knees, spreading out the map.)*

MAJOR PIKE. Over here you see Birmingham. Nashville. Chattanooga.

GENERAL. I don't like seeing an Army Major prowlin' around the floor like a possum.

*(***PIKE** *stands up.)*

MAJOR PIKE. Sorry, sir. Now, northern Alabama is here….

GENERAL. And I don't need a lecture on Southern geography. I'm a proud son of Lookout Mountain, Tennessee.

(The **GENERAL** *points down to his hometown on the map.)*

MAJOR PIKE. Then as you would know, here is the Tennessee-Alabama border.

GENERAL. *(an irate order)* You take off your shoes when you walk on Tennessee!

*(***MAJOR PIKE** *does so.)*

MAJOR PIKE. Yes, sir. South of the Tennessee border is the Redstone Arsenal – right there, in a little Alabama town called Huntsville. Population sixteen thousand, four hundred and thirty seven. The missile construction facility would be right here.

GENERAL. And who we got building these missiles?

MAJOR PIKE. Fortunately, the greatest rocketry mind in the world. Dr. Wernher von Braun and his team.

(PIKE, fluent in German, pronounces the name accurately: "VEH-nah fahn BRAH-oon." with a slight roll in the R in Von Braun.)

GENERAL. Those Nazi scientists we captured?

MAJOR PIKE. As I said, sir, the best in the world. During the war, while we invented the A-bomb, they invented the guided missile.

GENERAL. And you're going to park these Nazis in an all-American southern town? Not in my army, and not in my South!

(Lights down on the military men, lights up on ISRAEL WATKINS, an African-American blues singer, wearing classic bluesman attire: a dark suit and open-collar white shirt. He sits in a chair playing guitar; performing in semi-limbo, with perhaps a suggestion of a juke joint / blues club.)

(ISRAEL, in his first two scenes is a vague figure, perhaps part of the play, perhaps an observer or a theatrical "device." It isn't until he meets AMY (Act One, Scene 9) that he is perceived as an actual character in the play.)

(ISRAEL plays and sings the traditional blues song: "Alabama Bound," up tempo, with a blues guitar train rhythm. He sings with excitement and anticipation.)

ISRAEL.

I'M ALABAMA BOUND
I'M ALABAMA BOUND
AND IF THIS TRAIN
DON'T STOP AND TURN AROUND
I'M ALABAMA BOUND

(ISRAEL plays a "train" riff on the guitar that segues into the real sound of a moving train.)

Scene Three – An Alabama-Bound Train

(Lights up on the inside of a train, two women sitting side by side in their seats.)

*(**AMY LUBIN** of the Bronx is 21, dressed casually in her individual style that owes very little to the fashions of the moment, other than a touch of Greenwich Village bohemian. Certainly no bobby-soxer nonsense for this sharp college girl.)*

*(Next to her, is **SUSANNA PRUITT**, a middle-aged, wealthy, well-educated, Southern society woman. She wears a stylish traveling outfit, worthy of the New York fashion magazines she reads. And she makes sure she dresses five percent, not fifty percent, better than the ladies in her Alabama social set. If Susanna has some "country gal" mannerisms, they are carefully chosen affectations, like the gold banjo brooch she is wearing.)*

*(**AMY** is asleep. **SUSANNA** is reading some newspaper clippings she keeps in her purse.)*

*(**AMY** stirs.)*

AMY. *(a yawn)*

*(**AMY** wakes up and stretches her arms wide and fast. She accidentally slams the back of her hand into **SUSANNA**'s face.)*

SUSANNA. Oh!

AMY. Oh God, I'm SO sorry! I hit you right in the face! Did I hurt you?

SUSANNA. Well, my make-up might be mussed. But don't you worry, I brought my little tool chest.

AMY. I'm really sorry. When I fell asleep, there was no one sitting there.

*(**SUSANNA** pulls out her compact and begins repair work.)*

SUSANNA. Don't you spit beans over it. I'll be all patched up by the time we get to Alabama. That where you're getting off?

AMY. Yes, I'm Alabama bound!

SUSANNA. Just how I was born.

AMY. Excuse me?

SUSANNA. Alabama bound. On a Pullman sleeper heading south from Tennessee. Mama was coming home from Aunt Carol Jean's in Knoxville and I popped out a bit ahead of schedule.

AMY. Really! Now, your cheek – you're sure you're OK?

SUSANNA. Oh, honey. I've deserved to have my face slapped many a time. And at what town are you gettin' off?

AMY. Huntsville.

(**SUSANNA** *slaps* **AMY**'s *arm lightly.*)

SUSANNA. Don't tell me! Don't you tell me! That's where I live. Where I was born!

AMY. I thought you said you were born on a train.

SUSANNA. I was. But officially, it's Huntsville. You see, that train was still over the state line when I was born and they were gonna write "place of birth, Tennessee" on the birth certificate. Tennessee? Well, Mama wouldn't hear of it!

(**AMY** *laughs at that.*)

SUSANNA. And where were you born?

AMY. New York City. A section called the Bronx.

SUSANNA. *(what a word!)* The Bronx! Isn't that a lovely name.

AMY. Oh, the name might not be all that lovely, but that part of New York is. There are parks and ponds. And a street called the Grand Concourse that looks like a boulevard in Rome.

SUSANNA. Well, I've seen Rome, on our honeymoon. And Paris and Venice – We were invited to dinner there by a contessa.

AMY. Oh, it sounds wonderful! Me, I've never even been out of New York before.

SUSANNA. Is that so? And what could be bringing you all this way?

AMY. My Alabama fiancé. We met in New York. He was there for a reunion of his pilot buddies from the war. And one of those buddies lived on my floor.

SUSANNA. He lived on your *floor?*

AMY. No, I mean the same floor of my apartment building. Third story up. Across the hall.

SUSANNA. A third story love story. And what's the name of your young man? I'm sure I know the family.

AMY. Jed Kessler.

(SUSANNA playfully slaps AMY's arm again. Maybe a touch too hard.)

SUSANNA. Don't tell me! Don't you tell me! Of course, I know Jed Kessler! Ruth and Martin's boy. They live on Ashburton Street and Martin has the appliance store on the courthouse square. They go to the Jewish church on Chestnut Street.

AMY. Yes, that's my Jed. The Jewish churchgoer.

SUSANNA. And you attend a church of that denomination in the Bronx?

AMY. Not really. I mean, yes, I'm Jewish. But not much of a churchgoer you might say. You probably know more about Jed's family than I do.

SUSANNA. Oh, darlin', in Huntsville, I make it my business to know everyone. But I'm no busybody, it's professional interest. I'm Susanna Pruitt. I write the social column for the Huntsville Courier.

AMY. I'm Amy Lubin. So look at this, I'm meeting a newspaper columnist.

SUSANNA. Oh, wasn't such a hard job to get. My husband Lester owns the paper.

AMY. Still – you're a genuine writer.

SUSANNA. English major at Bama.

AMY. Bama?

SUSANNA. University of Alabama. I graduated Class of…did you really think I was gonna tell you what year?

AMY. *(friendly flattery)* Last year?

SUSANNA. Oh, I knew I was gonna like you! For my senior thesis, I wrote and published a book on local history. "Home Sweet Huntsville." I'll send a copy to you at the Kesslers.

AMY. Oh, so nice of you, Mrs. Pruitt.

SUSANNA. *(with a smile)* "Susanna" will do just fine. And I bet after hearing my story, you can guess why my Mama named me that.

AMY. No, I can't guess…

SUSANNA. *(giving a hint)* Well, I was comin' to AL-a-bam-a…

(AMY still doesn't get it. Then:)

AMY. Oh, yes! "Susanna!" Do you have a banjo on your knee?

SUSANNA. No, but I got one on my booby! See this gold brooch? Banjo-shaped. Twang twang. Now don't you hate me, Amy-from-New-York, but I've just got to put something about you in my column. Has your engagement been formally announced?

AMY. As formally as we do things in the Bronx. Which is to say, my mother screamed the news out the window.

(SUSANNA takes AMY's hand.)

SUSANNA. Then why don't we make the formal announcement in my column? But till then, we'll keep it our little secret, all right? We have ourselves a deal?

AMY. Sounds fine. If that's the way things are done.

SUSANNA. Oh, we're gonna be good friends, I know it. I adore Jed. He'd get the blue ribbon in the handsome bake-off, that's for sure.

AMY. It would go nicely with his bronze star.

SUSANNA. Bless his heart, winnin' the war for us. *(pointing out the window)* Oh, lookit out the window, there's the state line. Mama and I would sing our little song whenever we crossed over to Alabama.

AMY. You know, I bet I can guess what the song was.

SUSANNA. I'm gonna call you my froggy-girl, 'cause you're always two jumps ahead. *(singing)*

OH I COME FROM ALABAMA

…Sing along!

*(**AMY** joins in, awkwardly. No accompaniment)*

AMY & SUSANNA.

WITH A BANJO ON MY KNEE

AMY.

AND I'M GOIN' TO LOU-EEZ-EE-ANA…

SUSANNA. *(all too quick to correct her)*

LOOZ-EE-ANA

AMY.

"LOOZ-EE-ANA," MY TRUE LOVE FOR TO SEE…

SUSANNA. Lord, we know who she means!

MY TRUE LOVE Jed-Kessler GONNA SEE

OH SUSANNA…

AMY & SUSANNA.

OH DON'T YOU CRY FOR ME…

*(Light up on **ISRAEL** who picks up the song on guitar and voice, bluesing it up. He sings at the same time the women are singing "Oh Susanna.")*

ISRAEL.	AMY & SUSANNA.
DON'T YOU CRY FOR ME	FOR I COME FROM ALABAMA
DON'T YOU CRY FOR ME	WITH A BANJO ON MY KNEE

ISRAEL. *(now singing alone)*

AND IF THIS TRAIN I'M ON

DON'T TURN AROUND…

*(Lights back up on the **GENERAL** and **MAJOR PIKE** as **ISRAEL** sings.)*

I'M ALABAMA BOUND

I'M ALABAMA BOUND

(Solo guitar underscoring segues into next scene.)

Scene Four – General Barklee's Office

GENERAL. So, Alabama's where you want 'em. Where you got these Krauts stashed right now?

MAJOR PIKE. West Texas.

GENERAL. Well, let 'em build rockets with the rattlesnakes. Be among their own kind.

MAJOR PIKE. Without the Redstone Arsenal, we would have to build a missile facility from scratch. That step alone could take a year or two. Which is why I am requesting the Redstone. It produced artillery shells during the war. I want it re-tooled for the manufacture of missiles.

GENERAL. But these men built rockets for Hitler!

MAJOR PIKE. These are not Nazis, General. These are men of science.

GENERAL. You expect that Alabama town to buy that? What do you think, we're all just a bunch of dumb, thick-neck cotton-choppers? Typical Yankee mentality.

MAJOR PIKE. I'm from Virginia myself, sir.

GENERAL. Where?

MAJOR PIKE. Alexandria.

GENERAL. That's Yankee Virginia! Bedrooms for the Washington blowhards. I'm talking about the proud South, that sent and lost her sons in a war with the Japs and the Germans.

MAJOR PIKE. The alternative is building a new facility. And how long will that take, just to get the funds out of Congress? And while the "blowhards" are pushing for their home district, the Russians will be perfecting their missiles.

GENERAL. But these are Nazis!

MAJOR PIKE. I was there, sir, a first lieutenant with the 44th Infantry Division in Austria. I was there, when these men surrendered to us. I know German and I quickly found out what a treasure we had in our hands.

GENERAL. And I see you ain't let them OUT of your hands. Gonna make your reputation on this missile program? Got political ideas like General Eisenhower?

MAJOR PIKE. I'm doing what's right for our country.

GENERAL. By sneakin' Nazis into it. How'd you ever pull that off, anyway?

(This signature process is taking too long. **MAJOR PIKE** *decides to play his ace.)*

MAJOR PIKE. You might have heard of my father? Hamilton Pike, Senior?

GENERAL. The Washington lawyer.

MAJOR PIKE. Well, he has some clients high up in the State Department and they were kind enough to help us with the visas.

GENERAL. Political influence. Always wins the battle.

MAJOR PIKE. *(coming in for the kill)* Yes, Ham Senior has some Pentagon honchos as clients, too. *(a threat as a joke)* Our big bosses way upstairs! Me, I'd never get to shine the shoes of the *(pointedly)* head of the army, and dad's playing a round of golf with him.

*(***PIKE*** *pauses as his threat sinks in.)*

But, if I may continue, sir. The German scientists we're speaking about chose America. They want to serve our country. And help us prevail against the Russians.

(a beat)

GENERAL. Major Pike – is what you're saying true?

MAJOR PIKE. It has some truth in it.

(a beat)

General Barklee, sir, I promised the President I would deliver him an American guided missile system and soon. As we talk here, the Russians may be already test-launching their first missile. And they may have a map exactly like this, with a circle around that secret radar station on *(indicating a spot on the map with his foot)* Lookout Mountain, Tennessee.

(The **GENERAL,** *a good soldier, knows when he's defeated.)*

MAJOR PIKE. Your signature, sir?

*(***MAJOR PIKE** *pushes the document in front of the* **GENERAL** *who hesitates and signs it.)*

GENERAL. The Redstone Arsenal is all yours. *(bitterly)* Congratulations. Or should I say Sieg Heil.

(Lights fade on the General's office. Lights up on **ISRAEL WATKINS,** *singing the lines of "Oh, Susannah," blues style then segueing into "Alabama Bound.")*

ISRAEL.

DON'T YOU CRY FOR ME
DON'T YOU CRY FOR ME
'CAUSE I'M ALABAMA BOUND
ALABAMA BOUND
AND IF YOU WANT MY LOVIN' BABE
YOU GOT TO LEAVE THIS TOWN

(As **ISRAEL** *is singing, lights up on* **MAJOR PIKE** *at his desk in his new office. He unpacks his briefcase and the map we saw. Out of his briefcase, he takes a small American flag and places it on his desk. Next, he takes out a matching Confederate flag, places it next to the American flag. He's ready for Alabama.)*

(Guitar chord buttons scene.)

Scene Five – Front Porch Of The Kessler Home

(Dark stage and the sound of a rhythmic squeaking.)

(Lights come up slowly. It's nighttime on the Kessler porch. AMY and JED are sitting on a porch glider which is squeaking as they move it with their feet.)

(Boyishly good-looking JED has a Southern boy's courtliness and style of speech, with a bit of devilishness in him.)

AMY. *(romanticizing)* Listen to that chirping. Is that some kind of Alabama bird or something? One that only sings at night?

JED. No, Amy, it's the glider squeaking.

AMY. *(her bubble burst)* So, what, no nightingales?

JED. Needs a little shot of oil. Here, stop moving it, sit still.

AMY. I still hear some squeaking.

(They listen to the chirping of cicadas.)

JED. Now, THAT sound is insects.

AMY. Crickets?

JED. Cicadas. You're in the South, now, honey. Where we drink sweet tea.

AMY. Oh, Jed, don't remind me! I found that out when I added sugar.

JED. Southern iced tea is sweet when it comes to the table.

AMY. Which is obviously why you call it sweet tea. But it looked like iced tea, so I just reached for the sugar. So polite, your mother, to let me pour in the sugar and not stop me. Or make fun of me.

JED. Oh, they all loved you. But you're not exactly a hard sell.

AMY. I didn't overdo it? I kept feeling I was interrupting your parents when they were talking to me. I tried to control that.

JED. Well, you did interrupt them, but you were just over-eager. They knew that.

AMY. No, it's not over-eager. In New York you're SUP-POSED to interrupt when people are talking.

JED. You are?

AMY. Oh, yes! It shows you have proper manners. If you don't interrupt people, they think you aren't listening to them. It's like telling them they're boring. Here try it – I'll keep blathering, and you interrupt me.

JED. I couldn't! You wait until someone finishes, then you start to talk.

AMY. Not in the Bronx. Come on – I'm gonna talk, you interrupt. *(beginning the exercise:)*
You know, your mother and Jewish words in a Southern accent, so funny! I nearly…

*(**AMY** gestures for **JED** to interrupt. He does his best.)*

JED. Good thing you held back your giggling. *(a beat)* How was that?

AMY. Good, but a little hesitant. Jump right in, don't wait until an appropriate moment. Yes, there's something about hearing a Southern accent on *(in "Southern")* "We were schleppin' ovah to shul on Rosh Ha-shanah" that just got me. I thought I was going to…

JED. *(interrupting)* Oh, funny to your New York ears.

AMY. Much better interruption!

JED. It still feels rude.

AMY. You'll get used to it… *(back to her instruction)* Then I just had to squeeze my teeth together when she got to "Yom Kipp-uh." Between the Jewish words in a Southern accent, me putting sugar in the sweet tea, my first taste of corn bread, and well, to make a long story short…

JED. It's already too long.

AMY. Interruption with a wisecrack! Hooray, Jed! You'll be ready when we see my family again.

JED. They did interrupt a lot.

AMY. Yes, they don't even talk. They ONLY interrupt.

JED. This time I want you to finish. I'm not breaking in: Did you like them? You like it here?

AMY. Oh, they're like the tea, they don't need extra sweetening.

JED. Southern hospitality.

AMY. I'm sitting on a porch in the Deep South. The farthest I've been from home. I feel like I'm in some kind of Southern storybook – like I'm Scarlett O'Horowitz.

JED. You sit outside like this on a spring night in New York?

AMY. Maybe on the fire escape. On really hot nights, my brother and I used to sleep out there.

JED. We could sleep outside here – or how's about up on Monte Sano hill? *("Monty Sann-o")*

AMY. And what would your mama think about an overnight like that?

JED. I'll tell her it'll be just like the Biltmore Hotel up in New York.

AMY. That was different. I'm a Southern Belle now, and we don't do such things until we're married! *(in a Scarlett O'Hara manner)* Whah, the very i-dea!

JED. Begging your pardon, ma'am.

(**JED** *pulls her back down into the glider. More sliding, more squeaks.*)

JED. Sounds like the bedsprings at the Biltmore.

AMY. Jed! *(She gets up.)* Oh, our house has to have a porch like this.

JED. It will. I got my eye on a house with a porch on every side. Tulip trees and cottonwoods all around. *(sound of charm bracelets)* Oh no. Do you hear that?

AMY. Hear what?

JED. That's Mrs. Dupray, my old piano teacher.

AMY. Jed, you play the piano? You never told me!

JED. Play it? After lessons with that woman, I can barely LISTEN to a piano without gettin' the shakes.

(MRS. DUPRAY enters, fanning herself with her hanky, setting off the clanging of her charm bracelets. She is a middle-aged Southern woman with excruciatingly good manners and diction.)

MRS. DUPRAY. Good evening, Jed. Beautiful sky tonight, isn't it?

JED. Yes, indeed, Miz Dupray. Beautiful sky. Amy, this is Miz Dupray. And this is Amy, from New York, who I'm gonna marry.

MRS. DUPRAY. Yes, I read all about you in Mrs. Pruitt's column. Oh, Huntsville is a long stretch from the cultural life you're used to. I tell all my students...

AMY. ...yeah, I know, you were Jed's piano teacher! Oh, sorry to interrupt.

MRS. DUPRAY. Not at all. *(but she did not like being interrupted)* As I was beginning to say: My music students, Dear Lord, I'd have to take them down to Birmingham to hear a real orchestra play. You remember those trips, Jed?

JED. *(cringing at the memory)* Every one of them!

MRS. DUPRAY. But then, we'd return to this cultural Death Valley.

AMY. I once saw Stokowski conduct.

MRS. DUPRAY. Isn't that lovely! Not too many in this town who'd appreciate that story. I hope you won't think ill of us.

AMY. Oh, no, really, no. Everyone's been wonderful.

MRS. DUPRAY. And it's just wonderful to have you here. Now, I have some Stokowski recordings, if you'd ever like to come by and have a listen. The Beethoven Piano Concerti. Complete.

AMY. We'll be glad to, won't we, Jed?

JED. *(but horrified)* Oh, yes! Absolutely!

MRS. DUPRAY. I'll make some lemonade and ginger snaps and we'll have ourselves a regular musicale. Good night, now.

AMY AND JED. Good night, good night, Miz. Dupray.

>*(MRS. DUPRAY* clanks off.*)*

JED. Quick, quick, I have to kiss you.

AMY. What?

>*(JED* kisses her fully.*)*

AMY. What was that?

JED. I knew that little hen would be peekin' back over her shoulder. I wanted to give her somethin' to cluck about.

AMY. Well, I guess she got what she needs.

JED. We have to be very sure about that…

>*(JED* kisses her again. Lights go down on the squeaking of the glider. Music transition: Solo guitar "Oh, Susannah." Music fades out as next scene begins.*)*

Scene Six – Major Pike's Office

(Lights up on **SUSANNA PRUITT** *and her salt-of-the-earth husband,* **LESTER,** *a self-made businessman from Alabama farmer stock. They are entering the office of* **MAJOR PIKE,** *who stands to greet them. The major's map of the area is prominent on the wall.* **PIKE** *shrewdly affects a slight, just-Southern-enough accent.)*

MAJOR PIKE. I'm Major Hamilton Pike, Jr. My thanks for coming in, Mr. Pruitt. Mrs. Pruitt.

*(***SUSANNA** *instinctively pours on the charm for this attractive man in uniform.)*

SUSANNA. Our thanks for inviting us. I must say, the young gals around town have been noticing you, Major Pike. And they're wonderin' if you're single.

MAJOR PIKE. *(with a wink)* I am. But perhaps not for long, what with all these lovely Southern ladies catchin' my eye.

LESTER. Could we get to the point here?

MAJOR PIKE. Certainly, Mr. Pruitt. You might have heard that I'll be addressing the town leaders tomorrow night.

SUSANNA. Yes, in our hotel ballroom. About all the big changes comin' to Huntsville.

MAJOR PIKE. Yes, ma'am. And I just wanted to make sure I had some friends in my corner.

SUSANNA. And you chose US? Hear that Lester?

MAJOR PIKE. Well, Mrs. Pruitt, you are a leader of Huntsville society. Influential columnist of the Courier. And Mr. Pruitt, you own the newspaper and many, many acres of farmland in this county.

LESTER. *(impatient)* Word is you want to expand the Redstone Arsenal. Turn our little town into an army base. Saloons. Tattoo parlors. Women of dubious repute.

SUSANNA. Lester!

(**PIKE** *is a natural and effortless performer and sales-man. He paints the picture vividly, with expansive gestures and heightened speech.*)

MAJOR PIKE. Yes, we'll be expanding the arsenal. But not into a barracks town. Huntsville is going to be the center of rocketry for the entire free world. "Rocket City, U.S.A." What Detroit is to cars, what Pittsburgh is to steel, Huntsville is gonna be to guided missiles.

(**SUSANNA**, *the columnist, takes a pad and pencil out of her purse and begins taking notes.*)

SUSANNA. Now, is it rockets or missiles y'all will be manu-facturing here?

MAJOR PIKE. One and the same, Mrs. Pruitt, depend-ing what's attached to the tip. They're missiles when they're defending our country and rockets when they are exploring outer space. Think of it, Mrs. Pruitt – rockets from Huntsville, traveling to Mars.

SUSANNA. Hear that, Lester? Rockets to Mars! I'd like to be on the first one!

(**LESTER** *stares at her and grunts.* **PIKE** *knows* **SUSANNA** *will be easy to win over. He begins working on* **LESTER**.)

MAJOR PIKE. And as the arsenal expands, this county will have a real estate boom that will make Alabama history.

LESTER. *(the real estate mogul)* Is that so. Which areas of the county you gonna develop?

MAJOR PIKE. *(tantalizing him)* Well, I can't say exactly, sir. Some local speculators would start buying up cheap land tomorrow and then sell it back to the govern-ment at a huge profit.

LESTER. *(wheels turning)* Would they?

(**PIKE** *sees he's got* **LESTER** *on the hook.*)

MAJOR PIKE. But, speaking Southerner to Southerner – I'm from Virginia myself – I'm worried about some of our scientists who'll be working here. And here's where I need your help at the ballroom meetin'. I want to make sure they're accepted.

LESTER. Oh, Lord, I knew there'd be a catch. What are they, foreigners?

SUSANNA. Stop it, Lester, maybe he just means Yankees.

MAJOR PIKE. The truth is, they're from Germany.

*(With that word, **PIKE** loses them both.)*

LESTER. KRAUTS! Here? I'd rather have the women of dubious repute!

SUSANNA. We have a son who fought in the war, Major. Came home safe, thank the Lord.

*(**PIKE** squelches their response quickly and craftily.)*

MAJOR PIKE. See, that's the kind of misunderstanding I'm worried about. These rocket engineers fled the Nazis and came over to our side. Their leader is the greatest rocket scientist in the world, Doctor Wernher von Braun. *(Dumbing down his German, **PIKE** says "Von BRAHN.")*

Son of a European baron. Why, at 22 he had his doctorate in rocket science when there was hardly any of it to study. Invented most of it himself! When the war came, the Nazis forced him into service, but luckily for us, he jumped over to our side.

*(Socially-aware **SUSANNA** heard one word: "Baron.")*

SUSANNA. Major, may I ask a question? If his daddy was a baron, does that make HIM a baron, too?

MAJOR PIKE. I suppose it does.

SUSANNA. And does the Baron have a Baroness?

LESTER. Now what kind of pinhead question is that? You fixin' to marry him?

*(But **PIKE** noticed **SUSANNA** sparking to the European titles.)*

MAJOR PIKE. Oh, yes, the Baron and Baroness will be taking up residence here, with their two small daughters.

SUSANNA. My goodness, I'd certainly like to introduce the Baron and Baroness to some real Southern barbecue.

LESTER. Watch out, Major. When she starts her "li'l Southern Belle" routine, she's readyin' for battle.

MAJOR PIKE. *(ignoring him, to* **SUSANNA***)* But, yes, that's just what I'm hopin.' That you'll help this family – and all these immigrant families – enjoy what folks like us call Southern Hospitality.

LESTER. But didn't we just fight a war against them German sons of bitches?

MAJOR PIKE. And we won it, thanks to the courage of soldiers like your son. I myself saw combat with the Germans. 44th Infantry Division. So you can be sure I know the difference between Germans, good and bad. To get back to your question, Mr. Pruitt. We'll be expanding out from the Redstone Arsenal in several directions…

LESTER. Oh, yes, the land development. And which areas…?

MAJOR PIKE. Can't really talk about classified information. Though *(with a wink)* I s'pose I could point to the area on the map. That ain't really talkin' is it?

(Tantalizing **LESTER***,* **MAJOR PIKE** *holds his finger above the map, not quite pointing to a specific place. Yet.)*

MAJOR PIKE. And after all, y'all are doin' me a big favor, backin' me up tomorrow night at the town meeting, 'cause now you two understand the truth about the situation. And you'll help me explain about these German war refugees and their children, won't you? Perhaps a word in your column, Mrs. Pruitt?

SUSANNA. Of course, Major. With a headline. "Howdy-do, Your Highness! Huntsville is Home to Royalty." And why don't we arrange an interview with the Baron and Baroness?

MAJOR PIKE. Yes, ma'am!

*(***PIKE** *salutes her, though he intends nothing of the sort. Yet.)*

MAJOR PIKE. And you, Mr. Pruitt? Can I count on you to help your country?

LESTER. Yes, yes. Now, you were about to point out...

(**LESTER** *bends forward towards the map as* **PIKE***'s hypnotic finger moves towards its target.*)

MAJOR PIKE. Of course! Now, we imagine the arsenal facilities will begin expanding westward, from...HERE.

(*Just as* **MAJOR PIKE***'s finger hits the map, lights come down on the office and up on* **ISRAEL WATKINS**, *with his guitar.*)

ISRAEL. Nice to see so many friends here tonight at Sleepy Joe's Juke Joint. Now, some of us been far away in that war. And when I was far away, I'd play this one, and the fellas, they'd ask me to play it again and again.

OH I'M A POOR BOY, A LONG WAY FROM HOME
POOR BOY BEEN TRAVELIN' SO LONG
UP COUNTRY ROADS AND DOWN CITY STREETS
AND OH LORD I LEARNED RIGHT FROM WRONG

(*Solo guitar music continues as underscoring, which fades as the dialogue in the next scene begins.*)

Scene Seven – Euvella's Hardware Store

(**HEINZ KLAUBER**, *one of the German rocket scientists, is standing at the counter. He is a nervous, slouching, squinting scientist in spectacles. He holds a large spray bottle of ammonia, a mop, cleaning fluid, and a pair of household rubber gloves. Behind the counter is Euvella, a Southern working class woman with an appropriate drawl. Usually friendly, she acts a bit chilly towards* **HEINZ**.)

EUVELLA. That going to be it for you?

(**HEINZ** *speaks in a thick German accent.*)

HEINZ. Yes, zat is all.

EUVELLA. Let me just get my pad and tote you up.

(**EUVELLA** *exits.* **AMY** *steps up to the counter holding a can of household oil. She smiles at* **HEINZ**. *Isn't one supposed to chat in the South?*)

AMY. All those cleaning supplies! I bet you just moved in somewhere, right?

HEINZ. Yes, yes, I did.

AMY. It's that first big clean that's the tough one. But at least it's the right time of year for spring cleaning.

(**HEINZ** *nods.* **EUVELLA** *re-enters.*)

EUVELLA. All right, that's for the ammonia, the mop, the cleaning fluid, rubber gloves.

(**HEINZ** *hands her some cash.*)

HEINZ. Here iss zih money. Good day.

EUVELLA. *(coldly)* And there's your change. You come back now.

(**HEINZ** *rushes out.*)

EUVELLA. Who they think they're foolin'? That gonna be it for you honey? Just that squirt can of oil?

AMY. Yes, that's it. What did you mean? Who they're foolin?

EUVELLA. Them Germans. Hardly say a word. Think we don't notice. You talk to them, they practically jump out of their skin.

(**AMY**'s *New York liberalism kicks in.*)

AMY. Oh, they probably don't like speaking because of their accents. In my building in New York, we have a family of war refugees from Germany.

(**EUVELLA** *pauses a moment to take in this girl.*)

EUVELLA. Everyone in town comes in my store and Ah ain't never seen you.

AMY. I've only been in Huntsville a few days.

EUVELLA. *(correcting the newcomer)* "HUHS-vull."

AMY. Excuse me?

EUVELLA. You want to get along here, you say "HUHS-vull."

AMY. "HUHS-vull."

EUVELLA. There you go. You come here visitin' family?

AMY. Family-to-be. The Kesslers. Jed and I are engaged.

EUVELLA. *(now brightening)* Oh, the blushin' bride! Ah read all about you! He's a right nice boy, that Jed. Ah remember him picking out screws and bolts when he could barely reach the counter. Building an airplane man with metal wings, he told me, can you imagine?

AMY. And then he flew a plane in the war.

EUVELLA. See, he became an airplane man himself! Well, Ah can't see that your Jed would be any much happier 'bout them Germans bein' here.

AMY. *(lecturing a bit)* You know, these people had to drop everything and flee from Hitler. I mean, learning a new language, new customs. We really have to look at it from their point of view.

EUVELLA. Flee from Hitler…? Honey, this bunch in town, they didn't flee from Hitler, they was pals with Hitler!

AMY. What?

EUVELLA. The army brought dozens of 'em here to build rockets. Just like they built 'em for their Fuhrer. And you just know that fuhrer wanted 'em built real good.

AMY. That can't be.

EUVELLA. Now all of them, and their families, they're planted here to build rockets for us. My friend Ello ween, her and Gus got the café over on Twickenham. Elloween put a sign in her window "No Germans served here." Lost her first husband in the war, so Ah don't blame her, no, not a bit.

AMY. For me, it was my brother.

EUVELLA. *(genuinely touched)* Oh, honey. It seems everybody lost somebody. Was he married, your brother? Leave any children?

AMY. Married, no. But he was engaged to an English girl he met in the war.

EUVELLA. What's your name, sweetie? Ah'm Euvella Todd. Of Euvella's Hardware.

AMY. "Euvella" that's pretty. I'm Amy Lubin.

EUVELLA. Well, you're a pretty thing yourself, Miss Amy. And you got an armful of sweetness in that Jed Kessler. *(gently teasing)* Even if he does send his gal down to the hardware store for oil!

AMY. No, this was my idea.

(**AMY** *takes some coins from her purse, ready to pay.*)

EUVELLA. Oh, no, you take that oil squirter for an engagement gift. Not the most romantic thing, I know but… say, what's this here? A bride shouldn't be frownin' that way. Come on, say, Ah'm gonna love it here in "HUHS-vull."

AMY. *(unconvincing)* I'm gonna love it here in HUHS-vull.

Scene Eight – Major Pike's Office

(Lights up on **PIKE** *with* **LEMUEL DECATUR**, *a diction coach, elegantly dressed and groomed.)*

MAJOR PIKE. Our mission is to make Dr. Von Braun presentable to the community at large and eventually, the country. And he's coming off a little too... *(***PIKE*** pauses before saying the word.)*
All right, I'll be frank and this word will not be repeated. He sounds like a Nazi in a war movie. Now some in Washington are telling me to put him to work in a basement somewhere and deny that he exists. But me? I say hide him in public and make him a star. You're this area's top speech and diction coach. But with this client, you'll be in the presence of one of the greatest scientific minds on earth. An Edison, an Einstein, yes, that brilliant, and yes, completely aware of his brilliance and his importance to us. So I ask you to be tactful as you work with this man.

DECATUR. *(a thick-as-molasses accent)* Wall, he cain't be worse'n some of those Hally-wood folks Ah've worked with. Lord have mercy, the tempuh-ment of these people!

MAJOR PIKE. Yes, my mother was an actress for a while.

DECATUR. Would I know her?

MAJOR PIKE. Just a few supporting roles. Met Dad, the big Washington lawyer, and goodbye Hollywood. Have you worked with any native German speakers before?

DECATUR. German immigrants. When the war came, they were in a hot-foot hurry to get rid of those accents. Didn't want anyone suspectin' them of spahn.

MAJOR PIKE. Spine?

DECATUR. SPAHN! Espionage, Major Pike.

MAJOR PIKE. Yes, of course.

DECATUR. I worked with the Schmidts of Chattanooga. Now they're the Smiths. And the Braunhausens of Savannah. We changed their name to Brown. We start with the consonants, that nasty giveaway W – V. "Ven I vas vorking in Vashington." We drill that and drill that and turn it into "WHEN I was WORKing…

MAJOR PIKE. Who were those Savannah people?

DECATUR. Formerly the Braunhausens. Now the Browns.

MAJOR PIKE. That's what I want. I want him to call himself "Von Brown" from here on in, not "Fahn Brah-oon." And turn that "Fair-nah" into "Werner." You can do that, can't you?

DECATUR. Depends how willing he is. Just chat with him naturally, and I'll observe him.

(**VON BRAUN** *enters. He is no geek of a scientist like Heinz Klauber.* **VON BRAUN** *is tall, movie-star handsome, with the straight back and the unapproachable superiority of the German aristocracy. A baron, indeed, as well as a rocketry genius. In his hand is a model of the Redstone missile. And yes, he speaks in that clipped, tight, German accent, rarely smiling.*)

VON BRAUN. Major. I haff something that vill please you, I believe.

DECATUR. (*reacting to* **VON BRAUN**'s *speech and manner*) Oh, Lord!

(**VON BRAUN** *smoothly hides the missile behind his back.*)

VON BRAUN. Who is zis person?

DECATUR. (*to* **VON BRAUN**) Ah'm so sorry. (*to* **PIKE**) You're right, he sounds just like a…

(**DECATUR** *makes two furtive Nazi salutes to* **PIKE**, *who ignores him.*)

MAJOR PIKE. Doctor Von Braun. May I introduce Mr. Decatur of Atlanta, Georgia.

DECATUR. Lemuel Decatur. Ah'm happy to meet you, Doctuh.

VON BRAUN. (*suspicious*) Who iss he?

DECATUR. Mr. Decatur is a friend of mine, very interested in the rocket program. Please feel free to show him what you have there. And to explain it to us.

VON BRAUN. Ziss is a scale model of the rocket vee are building as a successor to the V-2.

MAJOR PIKE. Tell us about that rocket, Doctor.

*(***VON BRAUN*** likes this suspicious situation less and less. He glares at* **DECATUR** *and goes on, having all the rocket information in his head. Contemptuously, he translates the metric measurements into "American" for* **DECATUR.** *)*

VON BRAUN. This will be the very first American guided missile. Total length, 21.13 meters. *(to* **DECATUR***)* Vitch iss sixty nine feet, four inches tall. Propulsion iss liquid oxygen and alcohol. Guidance system is inertial. Maximum speed vill be 5,650 kilometers – 3,510.747 miles per hour.

MAJOR PIKE. Development costs?

VON BRAUN. *(with a glance to* **DECATUR***)* Do vee talk about such zings?

MAJOR PIKE. He's a taxpayer – he's footing the bill.

VON BRAUN. Ninety two point five million dollars U.S. Zo far.

DECATUR. Lordy! All of that pouring into little ol' Huntsville?

MAJOR PIKE. A large part. Continue, please.

VON BRAUN. This is a highly accurate, liquid propelled, surface-to-surface missile capable of transporting atomic or conventional varheads against targets at ranges up to 375 kilometers or 233.014 miles. Easily the distance from vere ve stand to – Atlanta, Georgia. *(with a stinging smile to* **DECATUR***)* Should such a zing ever become necessary.

MAJOR PIKE. *(to* **DECATUR***)* Doesn't he explain things well?

DECATUR. Very clearly.

VON BRAUN. Ah, so Mr. Decatur iss here as our experiment.

MAJOR PIKE. Doctor Von Brown, you are going to be representing the rocket program to the public. And the public will tell their congressmen whether they should fund it. Mr. Decatur will help us in that regard.

VON BRAUN. How?

MAJOR PIKE. To be frank, he will help make you more presentable to the American public.

VON BRAUN. *(quietly offended)* More "presentable." Iss that an American idiom, a slang vurd I don't understand? Or do you intend to insult me?

MAJOR PIKE. We are only a few years past the war, Doctor. There is still strong anti-German sentiment in this country. In this town. I want you to be the public face of the rocket program, but, to be blunt, you cannot come off quite so German.

VON BRAUN. Zen I did not misunderstand. You vurr beink insulting.

DECATUR. If Ah may say, Doctor, Ah've worked with several German families during the war. You can check mah references with the Braunhausens of Savannah, the Schmidts of Chattanooga…

VON BRAUN. You teach people to speak correct English? I heff spoken English zince I vass a schoolboy and I can barely understand vahn vurrd you are sayink.

MAJOR PIKE. If we can remain civil, I have a proposal.

VON BRAUN. I am a scientist! I vill not be directed like some common dancing girl.

MAJOR PIKE. Doctor, my mother was an actress. And quite a gifted dancer.

(**VON BRAUN** *is truly abashed. He, an aristocrat, insulted someone's mother!*)

VON BRAUN. Major, I spoke out of my hat. Please forgive me.

DECATUR. Ah spoke "out of heh-yund" *("Hand.")* Speakin' without thinkin', speakin' rashly. As opposed to "speaking through one's hat" which is speaking foolishly or ignorantly.

MAJOR PIKE. Excellent correction. *(to* **VON BRAUN***)* You see, that wasn't all that painful, right?

VON BRAUN. I spoke out of *(maliciously imitating Decatur's drawl)* heh-yund.

DECATUR. Makes you inadvertently comical if you misuse the language like that. And a man in your position, Doctor, can not afford to look comical.

(That one stops **VON BRAUN***.)*

VON BRAUN. I zuppose zat is true.

MAJOR PIKE. You can see that Mr. Decatur could only be of help to our overall mission.

VON BRAUN. *(a demand)* I'd like to discuss zis in private.

DECATUR. You know where to get in touch with me, Major. A great pleasure…

MAJOR PIKE. No, just wait outside the office, please.

DECATUR. Certainly will.

*(***DECATUR*** exits.)*

VON BRAUN. I do not like surprises like that. I do not like zis kind of humiliation in front of a stranger.

MAJOR PIKE. I am planning public appearances. Speeches. Even some television. Yes, you are a rocketry genius. But you're in America now. It's not enough to be a genius, you must also be a star, because, as my mother says, there are special rules for stars.

(a beat)

VON BRAUN. I might be inclined to co-operate.

MAJOR PIKE. I know you well enough. There's something you want.

VON BRAUN. Since I've been here in Alabama, I feel like I am a criminal under house arrest. I vas freer to valk around in Texas, to go out and explore and zink.

MAJOR PIKE. I want to hold you back until you are completely prepared for the public. You're too important.

VON BRAUN. But ven I do go out, there are men following me. Not Army men.

MAJOR PIKE. FBI. Mr. J. Edgar Hoover, the head of the bureau, he doesn't trust you.

VON BRAUN. *(sarcastic)* Vot does he zink I'm doing? Secretly meeting vit your enemies?

MAJOR PIKE. He's more concerned that you're secretly meeting with your old friends.

(**VON BRAUN**, *a genius, knows when to be silent.*)

MAJOR PIKE. Mr. Hoover hunted down Nazis in this country during the war and he doesn't plan on stopping now. I'll do what I can, but the FBI is not part of the military. And even my father's influence has its limits. Anything else?

VON BRAUN. I am still not comfortable vit ziss sort of performink.

MAJOR PIKE. You'll get more comfortable. We all have the same intentions, after all. We simply don't want you to come off like…

(**MAJOR** *holds up a file from his desk as a threat.*)

MAJOR PIKE. *(pointedly)* …well, like an SS officer. At a war crimes trial. *(pause)* Or something.

(**VON BRAUN** *is silent again.*)

MAJOR PIKE. I know how busy you are with the rocket model, but do you think you could find some time to begin work with Mr. Decatur?

VON BRAUN. Per-hepps in about two veeks venn I finish zih next set of designs.

MAJOR PIKE. Or "per-hepps" tomorrow morning. "Zehn uhr morgen fruh." At ten o'clock.

(*The two stare at each other.* **VON BRAUN** *does not reply.*)

MAJOR PIKE. Now, would you please ask Mr. Decatur to come back in here?

(**MAJOR** *and* **VON BRAUN** *hold eye contact.* **PIKE** *won this round and* **VON BRAUN** *is not pleased. Lights down.*)

Scene Nine – Kessler Front Porch

(**JED** *is applying oil to the glider to stop the squeaking.*)

JED. Yes, they've been coming in for a while – for the rocket program. You hear all kinds of stories about them. Small town life.

AMY. Euvella, the lady in the hardware store, she wasn't telling stories, she wasn't making this up.

JED. Oh, from what I hear, the likes of Euvella were seeing Nazis in the cotton fields all through the war.

AMY. What do you believe?

JED. I believe, Scarlett, that this seat will be chirpin' no more.

AMY. Do you think that guy I saw in the hardware store was actually a Nazi?

JED. Well, he was or he wasn't. Lots of Germans were and didn't want to be.

AMY. But don't you want to know? I mean, these could be people responsible for the exterminations. For the concentration camps.

JED. I'm sick of fighting Nazis, Amy. I loved flying my plane, loved sailing through the clouds, but I don't miss dodging those shells. Now I'm a civilian sort of citizen, and pleased to be.

AMY. But Jed, after all that happened in the war, are we supposed to just…

(**AMY** *stops speaking as she notices* **ISRAEL** *enter, now dressed in his truck driver work clothes.*)

ISRAEL. Afternoon, Mister Jed.

JED. Oh, good afternoon to you. Come on over here and meet someone. Amy, this is Nettie's husband, Israel. You should hear him play guitar.

AMY. Happy to meet you.

JED. Amy's my fiancée, come all the way from New York.

ISRAEL. Well, ain't that fine. Congratulations.

JED. She's getting her first taste of Southern cooking through Nettie.

ISRAEL. It's New York City you come from?

AMY. That's right.

JED. Nettie's just about finished up. Do you want me to get her?

ISRAEL. If you'd just tell her I'm out in the truck, Mister Jed.

JED. I'll do that.

> (**JED** *exits.* **AMY** *speaks to* **ISRAEL**, *who is a little wary.*)

AMY. Ah…Israel? I just want to tell you…

ISRAEL. Yes?

AMY. Nettie's been very nice to me. Her pecan sandies – my new favorite.

ISRAEL. Fond of them myself.

AMY. I'd love to hear your music. Do you play in a club or something? Maybe Jed and I can come hear you some night.

> (*Friendly* **ISRAEL** *is suddenly solemn. She's going to come to a Black blues club?*)

ISRAEL. Well, yes, you talk to Mr. Jed about that. *(getting to safer ground)* Glad to hear you like Nettie's cooking. Ask her to whip up some of her spoonbread for you.

AMY. Spoonbread. I'll ask. Just to find out what it is.

> (**JED** *re-enters.*)

JED. Nettie's on the way.

> (**ISRAEL** *grabs the moment to leave and end the awkwardness.*)

ISRAEL. Yeah, well, I'll be out in the truck. Nice meeting you, Miss Amy.

> (**ISRAEL** *exits.*)

JED. He picks up Nettie after work sometimes, when they're going out to the church or somewhere.

AMY. I told him we'd go hear him play. He wasn't too enthusiastic.

(a beat)

JED. Amy, he plays in colored clubs. I'd like to go hear him, too, but that's not how it works.

AMY. I know, I saw the separate seating on the train, all that.

JED. *(sensing disapproval)* It's better than it used to be. My parents, their friends, they were always working against the lynchings. And the Klan. Look at Miz Dupray – she complains about the lack of culture, but she won't give music lessons to colored kids. It's the good people who'll help it get better.

AMY. I knew how things would be in the South. But I wasn't prepared for Hitler's rocket men to be living down the street.

JED. If I know the South, those Germans will live on their side of town and won't be mingling much.

AMY. I just think people should know. It should be out in the open.

JED. Too much on your mind. Come on, sit next to me. Let's see if them durn squeaks are gone, Scarlett.

(**JED** *puts his arm around* **AMY**. *Lights down on them and lights up on* **ISRAEL** *singing, playing guitar.*)

ISRAEL.
OH I'M A POOR BOY A LONG WAY FROM HOME
POOR BOY BEEN TRAVELIN' SO LONG
UP COUNTRY ROADS AND DOWN CITY STREETS
AND OH LORD I LEARNED RIGHT FROM WRONG

(**ISRAEL** *continues playing, a guitar solo underscore. A light comes up on* **AMY** *writing a letter on a distinctive looking stationery.*)

AMY. *(over music)* "To the Editor of the Huntsville Courier. There are rumors and whispers about the Germans who have recently arrived in town to work on the rocket program. We deserve to know the background of these scientists, whether or not they were involved in the Nazi rocket program…"

(Lights down on **AMY**.*)*

ISRAEL.

THOSE WOMEN UP IN CHICAGO TOWN
THEY LIKE THEIR WHISKEY STRONG
IT'S DICE AND DRINKIN' AND ASKIN' FOR MORE
AND OH LORD I LEARNED RIGHT FROM WRONG

(Solo guitar music continues as underscore. Lights up on **SUSANNA**, *holding* **AMY**'s *letter, reading aloud to* **LESTER**.*)*

SUSANNA. "If it turns out they were part of the Nazi war machine, they should be deported and prosecuted with the rest of the Nazi war criminals."

*(***LESTER*** *takes the letter from* **SUSANNA** *and keeps reading.)*

LESTER. "But if we Americans are expected to live beside these people, we are entitled to know the truth about their pasts."

(As **ISRAEL** *begins singing again,* **LESTER** *takes the letter from* **SUSANNA** *and exits. Lights down on* **SUSANNA**.*)*

ISRAEL.

OH I WAS BORN ON A GEORGIA FARM
AND THAT'S WHERE I BELONG
MY MAMA SHE CAME FROM NEW ORLEANS
AND OH LORD SHE LEARNED RIGHT FROM WRONG

(Solo guitar continues as underscore. Lights up on Pike's office. **LESTER** *stands next to* **PIKE** *as* **PIKE** *reads Amy's letter aloud.)*

MAJOR PIKE. "Nazi war criminals are still being found and brought to justice. And isn't it for the cause of justice that we fought the Nazis? Sincerely yours, Amy Lubin." *(to* **LESTER***)* Do you know this girl?

ISRAEL.

AND OH LORD I LEARNED RIGHT FROM WRONG.

(guitar chord button)

Scene Ten – Major Pike's Office

*(Lights up. **AMY** is sitting across from **PIKE**. In his hand, **PIKE** holds Amy's letter.)*

AMY. I wasn't expecting a response from the Army. I wrote that letter to the newspaper. How did you get it?

MAJOR PIKE. Well, I thought speaking directly, we could clear up this misunderstanding. I want you to know that the German scientists here were subjected to stringent review when they decided to join us. You can't imagine that we'd let citizens of a former enemy country immigrate without proper investigation. I can assure you that these men were not Nazis.

AMY. As I understand it, they were scientists working for Hitler. I would think that makes someone a Nazi. And possibly a war criminal. See, my brother Daniel was in Navy intelligence. A cryptographer.

MAJOR PIKE. Was he? Important job.

(a beat)

AMY. He died in the war.

MAJOR PIKE. I'm sorry to hear that. A loss for you. And a loss for the country.

AMY. And you know how he died?

MAJOR PIKE. How?

AMY. On a boat sunk by the Germans.

MAJOR PIKE. Terrible shame. It sounds like you two were close.

AMY. I think about him every day. About Daniel taking me to baseball games. Daniel showing me the best place to stand on the subway platform. How to sneak into a movie theater...

MAJOR PIKE. I have a sister myself.

*(**AMY** cuts her pretense.)*

AMY. ...and just how much to believe when the military speaks. Which is very little. So, was anything you told me about the German scientists true?

MAJOR PIKE. I assure you, these men were investigated.

AMY. And I was, too. Right?

> (**PIKE** *hesitates. Where he's from, girls aren't this sharp.* **AMY** *gets her answer from* **PIKE***'s hesitation.*)

AMY. And you knew all I told you about Daniel before I walked in.

> (**PIKE** *takes a moment to make a strategy decision – honesty, a rare tactic for him.*)

MAJOR PIKE. It was a torpedo from a U-boat that sunk Daniel Lubin's ship, the Jefferson, in the North Atlantic.

AMY. Yes. And I guess you know plenty about me.

MAJOR PIKE. Born in the Bronx, attended De Witt Clinton High School, Hunter College for two years and left. Thinking of finishing?

AMY. *(with a smile)* Good research. Yes, one of the best colleges in the city. I was thinking of teaching. Then I met my…well, that's all in there, right?

MAJOR PIKE. I was educated in the East, too. I'm fourth generation Princeton.

AMY. I'm first generation college. And you're from Virginia, son of a big Washington lawyer, an eligible bachelor.

MAJOR PIKE. …as you read in Mrs. Pruitt's column…

AMY. …and from the looks of this situation, you have your eye on an eventual political career, right, "Senator" Pike?

MAJOR PIKE. Well, that part wasn't in her column. You're a pretty bright girl.

AMY. "Bachelor" doesn't work in politics.

MAJOR PIKE. You're right, I'll need a proper wife. Mrs. Pruitt's been introducing me to some Southern Belles. *(with a smile)* Of course, she'd have to be as bright as a New York girl.

AMY. Major, are you trying to flirt me over to your point of view?

MAJOR PIKE. It's worked from time to time.

AMY. *(not buying)* My brother died fighting against Nazis like the ones you brought here. Now that you've sufficiently charmed me, let me ask you something. Was *anything* you told me about these German scientists true?

MAJOR PIKE. I can assure you, we have investigated…

AMY. *(interrupting)* It's all right, I'll find out for myself. You can hold on to this letter for my file. Which you might as well keep open.

*(**AMY** exits as lights come down.)*

Scene Eleven – Heinz Klauber's Home

SUSANNA. Knockity knock! Anyone home?

(**HEINZ KLAUBER** *appears wearing the rubber gloves he bought in Euvella's hardware store. One of his gloved hands holds the spray bottle of ammonia.*)

HEINZ. *(nervous)* Yes?

(**SUSANNA** *breezes in carrying a picnic basket. She's in her flirtatious "Southern Belle" mode that* **LESTER** *finds so annoying.*)

SUSANNA. My goodness what a lovely home! Oh, I see you're busy. I'm interruptin'.

HEINZ. *(suspiciously)* Who are you?

SUSANNA. I'm Susanna Pruitt, from the Huntsville Welcome Wagon. A bunch of us gals are givin' a how-d'a-do to our new neighbors. And whom do I have the pleasure of welcoming to Huntsville?

HEINZ. I am…Heinz Klauber.

SUSANNA. Well, greetings Herr Klauber. Or is it Doctor?

HEINZ. Doctor Klauber.

SUSANNA. See, I know all about you science fellas!

HEINZ. *(in an ex-Nazi panic)* VOTT do you know?

SUSANNA. That you're all doctors of something or other. Now, is Mrs. Klauber at home? Or should I say Frau?

HEINZ. No, she iss not at home. She iss shopping at zih Piggly Viggly.

SUSANNA. If I'd gotten here sooner, might have saved her a few items on her list! We gals, we made up baskets for each family with some of the German foods y'all must be pining for. *(hinting)* Ooh, it's kind of heavy.

HEINZ. Ah. Please sit down, Mrs. Pruitt.

(**HEINZ**, *gesturing, notices that he has rubber gloves on.*)

HEINZ. Excuse me, I vass disinfectink.

(**HEINZ** *removes his gloves.* **SUSANNA** *sits down and reaches into the basket.*)

SUSANNA. Let's see what we got. Oh! Looky here! I bet you missed this. A bottle of German riesling, all the way from a winery in – I can't even read that label without my glasses.

HEINZ. *(reading the label)* Napa, Cah-lee-forn-yah.

SUSANNA. *(breezing past that)* Oh. You know, I've sipped wine in Europe, and I know our little town can't compare to what y'all are used to, with your chateaus and your Bourdeaus. Must be especially hard for the Baron and Baroness.

HEINZ. Zih Baron?

SUSANNA. Baron and Baroness Von Braun. *("Bronn")* He is a baron, isn't he?

HEINZ. Von Braun? Ya, he iss, I zuh-pose.

SUSANNA. And his wife, how do you properly address her – "your grace?" Can't be "your highness."

HEINZ. I'm sorry, I do not know zis.

SUSANNA. Well, with y'all she probably goes by Dagmar or Hildegarde. Oh, what's this I'm finding in my Germany basket? Why it's a hollerin' big jar of sauerkraut!

(With a flourish, SUSANNA lifts a jar of sauerkraut from the basket then hands it to HEINZ.)

HEINZ. Zank you. It's very…beautiful.

SUSANNA. Oh, just a little nothin'. You know, I wanted to bring a Germany basket to the Baron and Baroness. But Major Pike said they weren't quite ready for visitors or interviews. I understand that. We don't have much royalty here, unless you count the Cotton Queen.

HEINZ. Who is she?

SUSANNA. Oh, it's a silly thing. Each year we have the Cotton Carnival and one of the girls is the Cotton Queen. Just one of those silly small-town things. *(She notices he doesn't bite. She hints more broadly.)* I hardly even remember much of it anymore.

(A beat as she waits for his question.)

HEINZ. And you vere der.. ?

SUSANNA. Oh, goodness, you found me out! So you might say I'm sort of local royalty, which is why I'm so set on meeting the Baroness. But you guessed my deep dark secret so you win a prize! *(digging in the picnic basket)* Oops, oops, oops! What have I got nibbling on my fishing hook? A trout? A catfish? No, it's a whole school of – bratwurst!

*(**SUSANNAH** pulls a string of sausages out of the picnic basket. She pushes the "lead" sausage towards **KLAUBER**'s face.)*

SUSANNA. WE call 'em hot dogs! *(puppy noises)* Yip yip yip yip.

*(**SUSANNA** hands over the bratwurst to **HEINZ**.)*

HEINZ. You are very thoughtful.

*(**HEINZ** takes the string of bratwurst and, finding no place to put it, drapes it around his neck.)*

SUSANNA. Oh. Well, now that the town's switchin' from cotton to rockets, I suppose we ought to be crowning a Space Queen. *(fishing again)* But I'm a little over-the-hill for that sort of thing.

*(A pause. The hint is so broad even **KLAUBER** gets it. He sits down next to **SUSANNA**.)*

HEINZ. No, no, you vould make a voonderful Space Qvin.

SUSANNA. Oh, you and your Continental charm. Do you mind if I ask you a few questions for my column?

*(**SUSANNA** takes our her pad and pen. **HEINZ** nervously fondles the bratwurst.)*

HEINZ. I don't know…vot sort of qvestions?

SUSANNA. I don't suppose you can talk about the secret projects you're working on – but maybe you can give us a little tiny hint?

*(**SUSANNA**'s charm is irresistible. **HEINZ** succumbs. He relaxes and begins to return her flirtations.)*

HEINZ. *(with a twinkle)* Ve are buildink rockets.

SUSANNA. *(kittenish)* Rockets to Mars?

HEINZ. *(flirting in his way)* Perhaps even far beyond Mars!

SUSANNA. Ooo! And tell me this: What's he really like?

HEINZ. *(suspicious again)* Who?

SUSANNA. You know, your high chief. Your fearless leader. The big cheese!

(HEINZ, anxiety inflamed, leaps to his feet.)

HEINZ. Ve never met him! Ve never knew him! He died in his bunker in Berlin!

SUSANNA. But didn't you say he was here? Working with you?

HEINZ. *(now near panic)* Here? IN AH-LAH-BAH-MA?!

SUSANNA. You told me Baron von Braun was your leader.

HEINZ. *(immensely relieved)* Oh, Von Braun! Yes, yes. I thought you meant – doesn't matter.

SUSANNA. And what's he really like? The Baron?

HEINZ. A vunderful man. A scientist, not a political man at all. A scientist. Never knew anyone in politics.

SUSANNA. And do you think you might be able to get a message to the Von Brauns? I'd just love to give 'em their first taste of fried chicken and gravy.

HEINZ. Ya, of course. Would you like to write a note or zumzing?

(SUSANNA smoothly pulls out a pink envelope.)

SUSANNA. Already wrote it! Now you won't forget to deliver it, will you?

HEINZ. I von't forget.

(Mission accomplished, SUSANNA gets up to leave.)

SUSANNA. And I'm so sorry I wasn't able to visit with your missus, but you'll send her my regards, won't you?

HEINZ. Yes, I will tell her you vurr here Mrs…?

SUSANNA. Susanna Pruitt. Author, society reporter, and now, Cotton Queen of Outer Space!

(SUSANNA launches herself out of the room with a rocket noise. Lights out.)

Scene Twelve – Kessler Home And Various Locations

(**AMY** *is talking on a telephone. Lights up on* **POLLY**, *an English woman in a military outfit.*)

POLLY. Oh, Amy, darling, I'm so glad you called. But first I have to tell you, I think of Daniel all the time. Don't you?

AMY. And talk to him, Polly. Out loud sometimes, like I'm a crazy lady.

POLLY. Two crazy biddies, that's us. You know, Amy, loving Daniel was the best thing to come out of that rotten war for me.

AMY. Polly, you can see – for Daniel, why I'm feeling how I do about these Germans, right?

POLLY. Yes, and good job most of what you're asking about is declassified here, since I'm still in the service. Out of cryptography, more into general intelligence gathering for Her Majesty.

AMY. Really! Have you met the Queen?

POLLY. *(teasing)* Met her? Darling, I SPY on her! (**AMY** *laughs.*) Now this is what you want to know about your German rocketeers. They made the V-1 missiles. Then the bigger ones – the V-2's. I know, after the atom bomb and Hiroshima, these weapons seem like toys. But at the time, the V-1 and V-2 were terrifying.

AMY. I was wondering what that V stood for.

POLLY. Vergeltungswaffe. *("Vehr-GEL-toongs-voff-fuh.")*

(**AMY** *snickers, despite herself.*)

POLLY. I know! German words sound so funny. You'd think as a people they'd be more giggly.

AMY. Vergeltungswaffe. And that means?

POLLY. Weapon of revenge.

AMY. And the rocket scientists? Were they Nazis?

POLLY. Well, you couldn't very well work up Hitler's secret weapons without being in the party. Von Braun's rank was major in the SS.

AMY. A major in the SS! Do you think he believed in what the Nazis did? The extermination of the Jews?

POLLY. Von Braun believes in Von Braun. He wants to build his rockets, whether it's Hitler or America footing the bill. The Americans focused on the atomic bomb during the war. The Germans built guided missiles. Now America needs missiles to deliver their A-bombs and the only ones who know how to build them are the Germans.

AMY. Von Braun and his staff. I was told that they escaped from Germany during the war.

POLLY. Oh, I wouldn't say escaped. When it was clear the war was lost, Von Braun scrambled his team out of their secret base in Germany and surrendered to the Americans. Good on him he did. If he'd surrendered to the British, we'd have strung him up for what he did to us. Cripes, every day there's a new book out about wartime London. Tuck into one of those for some first-hand reports.

AMY. I'll do that right away. Just in case they start removing that kind of book from the town library.

*(**AMY** picks up a book and begins reading. Lights up on* **SARAH***, an upper-class London woman. She begins telling her story casually, as if it were an anecdote at a party.)*

SARAH. At the time we lived on Gerald Road in Belgravia.

*(**AMY** reads the book's title aloud.)*

AMY. "London Pride – The City at War."

SARAH. It had been the boys and I, and my daughter, Lacey, since Edgar passed on. Lacey and I kept the home fires burning when the boys marched off to war. At first, she was in a snit, having to come home from school. A lot of bickering, but we settled in. As did all of our friends. Emerald Cunard (pronounced "*Koo-NAHD*") decided society must continue, and soldiered on with her dinner parties. It was Emerald who bested the American who said that war was hell. *(with an appreciative smile)* Emerald declared that war was vulgar.

(Light up on **BENJY***, a working class Londoner. He begins his story as if spinning a yarn to his mates at the pub. His tone darkens as he continues. Both stories become darker and more urgent as Benjy and Sarah relate them.)*

BENJY. We're still in that second-story flat in the East End – all fixed from the damage, it is now. I was too old to pick up a gun and go shooting Jerrys, so me and the missus, we kept on running our butcher shop, selling whatever we could get our hands on, which was none too much, I can tell you. But we did everything Mr. Churchill said, ran to the shelter when the sirens sounded, all of that. Oh, we got used to seeing German planes flying over – but when them doodlebugs come, well, that was something else again. The V-1's, officially, but doodlebugs or buzzbombs, that's what we called them bastards.

SARAH. They were terrifying, of course, but one had to, for at least a moment, admire the technical brilliance of the V-1. To build a bomb that could fly on its own. No airplane, no pilot. Something out of Jules Verne! There'd never been anything like it on Earth.

BENJY. They're sayin' about a thousand of those bleedin' bombs fell on London during the war. Blowin' up houses, blowin' up shops. Never forget the time I saw a black taxi door just hanging in a tree. And that sound. The noise of a V-1. Like a hum in your ear, like a fly. Then comin' on louder and louder till it's like a giant rattle, like a motorboat comin' at your head.

SARAH. Like an army shaking coins in tin cans.

BENJY. Then you'd look up, it was like a flying black knife.

*(***SARAH***'s tone grows solemn now.)*

SARAH. A great, awful, iron insect.

BENJY. Then it would get closer and you didn't think you could stand that bleedin' racket any more, but then you heard something worse.

SARAH. The silence. The terrible, terrible silence. Like all London was holding its breath.

BENJY. 'Cause when its engine stopped, that meant it was gonna drop down and explode.

SARAH. *(a light tone again)* My daughter Lacey called them, well, "farting fannies." Emerald was right when she said war is vulgar! But Lacey was a good girl – she took it on herself to be a warden. Looked smashing in the tin hat.

BENJY. When the doodlebug was flying, you'd yell at it, "Keep goin', you bastard," like you was at a horse race, "Keep goin', you bugger!" Shamed to say we'd feel relieved when we heard it explode somewhere's else.

SARAH. Lacey declared that a bomb ought to be dropped the proper way, by a pilot in a plane. *(lightly)* She said she didn't care much for the V-1 because it lacked the personal touch!

BENJY. Didn't make it to the shelter one night. I was soakin' my dogs in a footbath, relaxing a bit. Then I heard that bloody hummmmm. Hmmmmmm. I jumped up, quick-like, drying off me feet, but couldn't find me boots!

(Sound effect: The distant hum of a V-1. The noise gets closer, louder, louder – now turning into the deafening motor-boat rattle. Louder, louder still.)

BENJY. Keep going, you bloody bastard! Keep going!

*(The sound of the V-1 abruptly stops. Silence, as it falls from the sky. Neither **BENJY** or **SARAH** speaks during several extremely tense, silent, beats.)*

*(Then: Sound effect – BOOM! The V-1 hits. **SARAH** staggers.)*

SARAH. My windows were blown out, but I wasn't hurt, just frightfully scared. The explosion was outside, in the street. You see, it was always my sons I feared for, fighting in the front lines. But Lacey, she was on her way home – in her helmet, wouldn't you know, when the thing fell. I'd worried about the boys because it never occurred to me that I could lose a daughter in the war. But this was a different kind of war, wasn't it?

(Lights down on **SARAH**, *up on* **AMY**.*)*

AMY. *(reading)* But then came something even worse. The V-2. The V-1 was a basic flying bomb, but the V-2 was a much greater horror. Four stories high, with one ton of explosives at its tip. It could precisely pick a target. It could fly faster than sound. First it struck, and then you heard it coming.

(Lights up on **MAJOR PIKE**. *He's talking to a civilian whose back is to the audience.)*

MAJOR PIKE. Between us Southern boys – don't it make you smile to think the doorway to space is an Alabama cotton town?

AMY. *(still reading from her book)* Von Braun and his team had invented and constructed what was then the most powerful, most terrifying weapon in the history of warfare. They didn't just design the rockets, they designed the entire system for building them: an underground factory manned by slave labor from the nearby concentration camps.

(Solo guitar music underscoring sneaks in: "Alabama Bound.")

MAJOR PIKE. Sure, at first you'll be doing routine sketching. But really, there is no routine. None of this has ever been done before, which is what makes it so damn exciting.

(Light comes up on **ISRAEL**, *singing and playing guitar.)*

ISRAEL.
    I'M ALABAMA BOUND
    I'M ALABAMA BOUND

(The solo guitar underscores the following:)

AMY. In all, 937 V-1 rockets dropped on London and 164 V-2's. They killed or seriously injured over 28,000 Londoners. They destroyed nearly 30,000 London houses and damaged another million. Hitler's war was already lost when he launched most of the V-2's. It was simply a matter of causing as much death and destruction as possible before the inevitable surrender.

(**PIKE** *points to figures on a piece of paper.*)

MAJOR PIKE. That'll be your starting salary. And you'll be contributing to the defense of the nation while building a bridge to the stars.

ISRAEL.

AND IF THAT TRAIN
DON'T STOP AND TURN AROUND
I'M ALABAMA BOUND

(into solo guitar underscoring)

MAJOR PIKE. As far as your future and the future of the program, the sky, in this case, is not the limit – it's just the welcome mat.

(The man **PIKE** *is speaking to stands up to shake hands. We now see it is* **JED.**)

JED. Interesting. Tell me, Major, what made you think of calling me?

MAJOR PIKE. Ex-pilot and Huntsville boy. You know basic aeronautics and who's who in the area. All that makes you a valuable man to us, Jed.

JED. Can't deny that it does sound pretty damn exciting! But I couldn't sign on without discussing it with my fiancée.

MAJOR PIKE. Of course!

ISRAEL.

OH DON'T YOU THROW ME OFF
AND LEAVE ME HERE
I'M ALABAMA BOUND

(Definitive final guitar chord. Lights out.)

End Act One

ACT TWO

Scene One – Various Locations

(In dim light, we see members of the cast watching their television sets: **JED** *and* **AMY** *together.* **SUSANNA** *by herself.* **PIKE** *by himself. "From the TV" comes the voice of a Fifties-style announcer.)*

ANNOUNCER'S VOICE. *(offstage)* Tonight, like every Sunday night on the Disneyland program, we visit another section of the Disneyland Park in Anaheim, California. And tonight – well, tonight is tomorrow! That's right, we're going to travel to Tomorrowland and get a glimpse of the future of space travel with Dr. Werner Von Braun. *(Pronounced: "Werner von Brown.")*

(Lights now up on **PIKE** *in civilian clothes. He is looking at a Fifties-style TV set, which has its back panel side to the audience.)*

MAJOR PIKE. It's your night, "Werner." All the preparation and planning, tonight it could pay off. Tonight, America meets you on the most popular show on television.

(Lights full up on **AMY** *and* **JED** *watching their TV.)*

JED. Here, Nettie just made these pecan sandies. The cookies you like.

AMY. (**AMY***'s eyes are on the TV*) I'm not in the mood for a snack. Look, the screen just went blank.

JED. It's the weather. Sometimes when there's a thunderstorm, the television set blinks off.

AMY. Can we turn one of the knobs or something?

JED. Y'know, I can fly a P-51, but I can't work the controls of that thing.

AMY. Wait, it's back on.

JED. There he is.

AMY. Give me a cookie.

(Light up on **VON BRAUN** *on the set of a television show. He holds a model of a Redstone rocket, a larger version than the one he brought into Pike's office in Act One.)*

*(***VON BRAUN** *begins speaking. Yes, his accent has been altered and he no longer sounds like a war movie Nazi. The w/v problem has been almost corrected, but it takes some conscious effort on his part. He doesn't quite sound American, but could be taken for a Scandinavian or similar. He's been coached on smiling-for-the-camera too, though that also takes some effort.)*

VON BRAUN. Good evening. I am Doctor *(struggling with the W sound)* V-WEHRner Von BROWN.

(Light up on **SUSANNA,** *watching her TV.)*

SUSANNA. Lester, bring your bones in here! The Baron's on the television!

*(***LESTER** *enters, cocktail in hand.)*

LESTER. What's all this now?

SUSANNA. Isn't he dreamy?

VON BRAUN. Right now, man is taking his first steps towards the ultimate frontier – the conkWEST of outer space.

AMY. Can this be happening?

JED. Guess no Mickey Mouse tonight.

AMY. Just a Nazi rat.

(As he speaks, **VON BRAUN** *starts to tense, his voice getting away from him, increasing in volume with German intensity.)*

VON BRAUN. And the vehicle that will take us into space is this – the rocket ship. Many people *think a rocket to be a kind of firecracker!*

MAJOR PIKE. Relax, Werner, easy boy.

*(***VON BRAUN** *composes himself.)*

VON BRAUN. Some people think there is a big explosion that launches the rocket and it just sails through the air. And the early rockets, the ones invented by the Chinese, did really work like that, with gunpowder. But as rocket science advanced the rockets developed engines that would keep firing, keep burning, while the rockets flew through the air.

SUSANNA. I think *I'm* flyin' through the air!

VON BRAUN. This is a model of the first American guided missile which will soon be tested. It has an engine unit, right here, much like the one that powered the V-2.

AMY. He's talking about the V-2 like he's proud of it!

VON BRAUN. Just as the motor in your family car needs fuel, so does a rocket engine. And the rocket must carry its own fuel because *(as a forced-smile "joke")* there are no gasoline stations in outer space!

JED. Funny line.

AMY. Betcha he kept the Fuhrer in stitches.

VON BRAUN. Imagine a modern rocket to be an upside-down candle. Now, a candle's flame cannot burn without air, without oxygen. But there is no air in outer space. So how can the engine keep burning up there?

JED. Yeah, how?

AMY. JED!

VON BRAUN. You see, inside the rocket there are tanks of oxygen in liquid form.

*(**VON BRAUN** opens a panel in the side of the model rocket.)*

SUSANNA. *(smitten)* Oh, Baron! *I'm* gonna need oxygen!

LESTER. I like mine in liquid form.

*(**LESTER** takes a big swig of his drink.)*

VON BRAUN. *(gaining confidence)* The rocket carries its own fuel and oxygen which are fed through pipes into the engine, keeping the engine firing during the rocket's flight through outer space. With this new technology, man will be able to step into outer space, to aim for the stars.

AMY. Though occasionally hitting London.

MAJOR PIKE. And a star, "Werner," is what you just became.

ANNOUNCER. We'll come back to Tomorrowland in just a moment, after this word from your Nash Rambler dealer.

AMY. He built rockets for Hitler and now he's a tv star. The public will see him as a hero.

JED. You don't have a very high opinion of the public. There are a lot of ways to look at all this...

AMY. Oh, Jed.

JED. Listen to me, Amy, I just haven't found a good time to tell you something.

AMY. What?

JED. Your Major Pike. He got in touch with me and invited me out to the Redstone Arsenal.

AMY. What for?

JED. He had a little proposal for me. Something we should talk about.

(**JED** *wordlessly tells* **AMY** *his news, as lights dim on them and as another light comes up on* **ISRAEL**, *singing, playing guitar in his bluesman suit.*)

ISRAEL.

IT'S THE OLD SHIP OF ZION
IT'S THE OLD SHIP OF ZION
IT'S THE OLD SHIP OF ZION
GET ON BOARD, GET ON BOARD
GET ON BOARD, ALL MY SISTERS
GET ON BOARD, ALL MY BROTHERS
GET ON BOARD, EVERYBODY,
GET ON BOARD, GET ON BOARD.

Scene Two – Major Pike's Office

(Lights up on **AMY** *and* **PIKE**. **MAJOR PIKE** *is at his desk holding a leaflet in his hand. The map behind him is now cluttered up with memos, smaller maps, rocket design diagrams, etc. It's been busy in this office.)*

MAJOR PIKE. *(reading the leaflet)* "To investigate and expose the crimes of these Nazis." Your writing has gotten more forceful. I thought I explained the situation with these men.

AMY. You lied. You said they "decided to work for us."

MAJOR PIKE. They did.

AMY. They surrendered to us when the war was lost. They jumped from the sinking ship like rats. I want to see them on trial for war crimes.

(a beat)

MAJOR PIKE. You've been busy. Printing these fliers, leafleting at the arsenal gates.

AMY. Am I doing anything illegal?

MAJOR PIKE. It's a free country. That is, as long as we keep the Russians far away. And all the while, as I read in Mrs. Pruitt's column, you're picking out flowers and planning your wedding. Limitless energies. You're a rocket engine yourself.

AMY. American design.

MAJOR PIKE. Does your husband-to-be approve of what you're doing?

AMY. Jed? *(with an edge:)* Oh, you know he's considering that job offer.

MAJOR PIKE. *(deflecting with a smile)* Yes, he said he'd check with his fiancée. Good fella, that Jed. Knows his way around the sky. Knows the folks and the countryside. *(slight threat)* He'll rise high in the program if no one messes it up for him.

AMY. Yes, Jed and I are discussing the offer. You can understand that it's a private matter between us.

MAJOR PIKE. Good fella, that Jed. But this *(holding up the leaflet)* is a public embarrassment for me. People are asking questions, writing letters. I've worked my brain and charm to the limit changing the attitudes around here, and you are pushing back my clock. I made a promise to the President. To deliver him an American missile system to keep our nation secure.

AMY. Bringing ex-Nazis into the deepest workings of our most important weapons? That will keep the nation secure?

MAJOR PIKE. Did they not choose our country when they surrendered?

AMY. As opposed to surrendering to who? The Russians? England? I can imagine what the British would have done to Von Braun. And it wouldn't involve television time with Mickey Mouse.

MAJOR PIKE. *(with a smile)* Oh, you watched. He did well, I thought.

AMY. Too well.

MAJOR PIKE. It's another new science, television. Exciting, all the ways it can be used.

AMY. Selling detergent and whitewashing Nazis.

MAJOR PIKE. Nuremberg is over. The judges have all gone home.

AMY. There's a courthouse right in the middle of town. Perfect for a trial.

MAJOR PIKE. You'd have no case.

AMY. They were members of the Nazi party.

(**PIKE** *fires his shot.*)

MAJOR PIKE. But about to become American citizens.

(**AMY** *is stopped cold by that information.*)

AMY. No, they can't become Americans!

MAJOR PIKE. Can and will. I have friends high up at the State Department who helped me push it through. Quickly and quietly.

AMY. Making Nazis American citizens!

MAJOR PIKE. German scientists who were forced to work for the Reich. These men were not fanatical Nazis.

AMY. That's your defense? "Not fanatical Nazis?" They just built the bombs that dropped on London, set the city on fire, and their hearts weren't really into it, poor things? Von Braun was a major in the SS. He created an underground factory, using slave labor, working them in darkness and filth to build his damn rockets.

MAJOR PIKE. How did you – ? Oh, your brother's friends in Navy intelligence. *(a beat)* You know, they found a Japanese soldier last month on an island in Indonesia. Did you hear about it? He fired on his rescuers. He didn't believe the war was over.

AMY. Yes, and?

MAJOR PIKE. I'd say that soldier was like you. The war is over and another is in preparation. An atomic war that we must prepare for and avoid. The Russians are building missiles with atomic warheads. I figure their missiles, like the ones we're making, can travel about two or three hundred miles before going down. The next ones built – three or four hundred miles. We have to keep up. I want to have a missile that will reach Moscow before the Russians build one that will reach Washington. *(with a smile)* Or the Bronx. And Amy, do you know who they have designing their missiles?

AMY. I can't guess.

MAJOR PIKE. German rocketeers who worked for Hitler. Yes, the Russians captured a few. But I'll tell you what they don't have: They don't have Wernher Von Braun. And they don't have objections from their people. No one would dare speak out the way you do. And I'm determined to preserve that right for you in this country. So our missiles must be ready to shoot down their missiles over the Atlantic. Eventually, we will have our missiles in submarines and in underground silos all over the country. People will be at home, at work, in movie theaters – they won't even think about the missiles nearby, ready to be fired, ready to protect them.

AMY. That's insanity.

MAJOR PIKE. Maybe. But it's the future of warfare.

AMY. People won't let this happen.

MAJOR PIKE. If there's anything the last war taught us, Amy, people will let anything happen. World politics will be determined by what country has atomic warhead missiles and what country doesn't. And that's how it will be, until we invent something better. Or worse.

AMY. But why should Von Braun and the rest of them live here in luxury while other Nazis are in prison?

MAJOR PIKE. Oh, Amy, you know the answer: because we need them. They can do more for us in Huntsville than they could in a Nuremberg jail.

AMY. But it's wrong. It's morally wrong.

MAJOR PIKE. No, it's morally questionable. That's nothing I'd ever say to the general public, but I'll say that to you. Even good people must sometimes commit morally questionable acts. You see things in black and white, don't you?

AMY. Maybe I do.

MAJOR PIKE. I know a little bit about the movies from the inside. And they aren't black and white at all. They're really just darker and lighter shades of gray. During the war, it did seem like a black and white world. And now, a world of grays.

AMY. Not to me.

MAJOR PIKE. It's the post-war reality, Amy.

AMY. Then I'm not made for it. I still have to answer to Daniel in my conscience. Not just Daniel. All those lives lost in London and in Von Braun's rocket factories. This can't go unpunished.

Scene Three – Various Locations

(Lights up on **ISRAEL** *with his guitar. This time, he's dressed for church, wearing a shirt and tie, rather than his usual bluesman suit-with-open-collar outfit.)*

ISRAEL. Glad to see so many folks here at this Wednesday night prayer meeting. *(picking out someone in the audience.)* I haven't seen YOU here in a while. All right, then, I haven't been here in a while either. But when my Nettie tells me it's time for prayin', I put down my bottle and pick up my Bible. Nettie asked for this one, so here it is for you, baby.
THIS LITTLE LIGHT OF MINE
I'M GONNA LET IT SHINE
THIS LITTLE LIGHT OF MINE
I'M GONNA LET IT SHINE…

(Music becomes solo guitar, with "This Little Light of Mine" underscoring the following scenes. **ISRAEL** *might also quietly hum the melody behind the dialogue. A light comes up on* **SUSANNA***, writing a letter.)*

SUSANNA. Dear Baroness. It was so kind of you to write back and now I'm just itching for us to meet in person. I'm hoping you could attend a little ladies luncheon I'll be giving at my home… *(her mind running ahead of her writing)* …before any of those other "ladies" get their hooks into you. *(back to writing)* It would be so grand to have you there on the sixteenth at noon. Your new friend…hmmm. Yours sincerely. Hm, no. *(Aha!)* Your obedient servant, Mrs. Susanna Pruitt.

ISRAEL.
LET IT SHINE, LET IT SHINE,
LET IT SHINE

(Music goes to guitar instrumental underscore again. Light up on **DECATUR** *and* **VON BRAUN***.)*

DECATUR. Now the major wants us to work on how you'll approach the congressmen for more funding.

VON BRAUN. Yes, now I am to be a street beggar shaking my tin cup.

DECATUR. Call it what you want, Doctor, it's got to be done. Now Ah'm Congressman Porkbelly. Come in and greet me.

VON BRAUN. This person is my inferior, correct?

DECATUR. We don't have those in politics! Everyone's your friend! Now, come at me with your hand out like this and greet me.

*(**VON BRAUN** approaches, bows instinctively, then robotically extends his hand.)*

VON BRAUN. Good day, Congressman Porkbelly.

DECATUR. No, he's your chum! He's your old pal! Like this. "Hello Congressman! How do you do?"

*(**DECATUR** demonstrates, exuberantly grabbing **VON BRAUN**'s hand and shaking it while squeezing his shoulder with his other hand. **VON BRAUN** stiffens. **DECATUR** plows on.)*

DECATUR. "Now tell me, Congressman. How do you feel about beatin' the Russians to the Moon?"

*(**DECATUR** laughs. **VON BRAUN** tries to laugh with him, failing miserably. **ISRAEL** resumes singing.)*

ISRAEL.
THIS LITTLE LIGHT OF MINE
I'M GONNA LET IT SHINE...

*(Back to guitar underscoring. Light up on **EUVELLA**, wearing a slightly insane rocket-shaped hat on her head emblazoned with the name "Rocket City Hardware." In her hands she holds some potholders, also branded with the name of her store.)*

EUVELLA. Quiet down, quiet, shush now. Welcome y'all, to the grand opening of the new branch of my little hardware store. And the way things are getting built up around here, Ah may have to open a third branch. Can you imagine? Me, a business tycoon? So, thank

y'all for showin' up, c'mon and step inside and help
yourself to one of these free pot holders from "Rocket
City Hardware."

(**EUVELLA** *tosses out some "Rocket City Hardware" potholders to the audience as* **ISRAEL** *resumes singing.*)

ISRAEL.
THIS LITTLE LIGHT OF MINE
I'M GONNA LET IT SHINE
LET IT SHINE, LET IT SHINE
LET IT SHINE

(guitar chord button)

Scene Four – Rabbi Benjamin's Study

*(Lights up on the **RABBI**'s study. **JED** and **AMY** are already on stage as the affable, Southern-born **RABBI BENJAMIN** enters. His accent is light Southern; rabbinical training did not remove any pride in his roots.)*

RABBI. I wish I could give you a religious reason for bein' late. Fact is, I was takin' a nap!

JED. But dreamin' of heaven, right, Rabbi?

RABBI. You found the religion in it, Jed. And this must be your lovely New York fiancee. I'm Rabbi Benjamin. Big change for you, our little town, I'll bet.

AMY. Big change.

RABBI. Well, like Moses said, "I am a stranger in a strange land." That what you're feeling?

AMY. Just keeps gettin' stranger!

RABBI. Well, I'm from a big town, too. N'awlins. Only time I went north was for my training in Cincinnati.

JED. Oh, that's almost the South, Rabbi.

RABBI. I s'pose it is, if the breeze is blowin' from Kentucky.

*(**JED** and **RABBI** laugh. **AMY** isn't getting it.)*

RABBI. *(mock-mournful)* And how's your mama feeling about her son entering a mixed marriage?

AMY. Oh, no, it's not that. I'm Jewish.

RABBI. I meant…Southern and Yankee!

*(**JED** and **RABBI** laugh.)*

AMY. *(feeling duped)* Oh.

RABBI. *(still joking)* And your mama, a Daughter of the Confederacy!

JED. She wrapped herself in the rebel flag and went into mournin'!

*(**JED** and **RABBI** laugh heartily. Not **AMY**.)*

RABBI. How-EVUH will you raise your children?

AMY. *(sick of this)* As God-fearing Christians.

(RABBI and JED abruptly stop laughing. AMY smiles.)

JED. My Amy loves making jokes. Well, we have a list of things to discuss with you...

AMY. Some very serious.

JED. But let's start with the wedding service. First off, Mama was wonderin' how much Hebrew there'd be in the service.

RABBI. I take it she'd rather have less than more.

JED. She's concerned the ladies from her club won't understand a word.

RABBI. Tell her I'll keep the Hebrew to a minimum and translate for her non-Jewish friends and neighbors. *(starting his probe)* Do you read Hebrew, Amy?

AMY. No, I don't.

RABBI. *(with a smile)* No synagogue schools up there in New York City?

AMY. My parents – they're Jewish, but you might say left-wing politics is their religion.

RABBI. Have you adhered to their particular faith?

AMY. I never give that too much thought.

RABBI. Well, why don't you two join us on Friday evening? See how you take to a Jewish service. See how you like the Jewish life.

AMY. I feel I have been living a Jewish life.

RABBI. I mean with God.

AMY. My father used to say you don't have to believe in God to be Jewish.

RABBI. So you don't believe in God?

AMY. I believe in being Jewish. And one thing I'm feeling Jewish about is what's going on in this town.

RABBI. And what is that?

AMY. The Germans. I'd assume, as the town's rabbi, you'd be raising hell against this situation.

RABBI. We've discussed that within the congregation. The government has assured us that these scientists were all investigated and cleared.

AMY. That's what the Army tells you to believe. But I know that these men were the inventors of the V-1 and V-2 rockets. In England, they'd be on trial for their war crimes.

RABBI. And why is this so important to you?

JED. Well, I've been offered a job with the rocket program.

RABBI. I see. So what do you think about taking the job, Jed?

JED. I think it's what I've been looking for and didn't even realize I was. I figured my life after the war would be selling washing machines and TV sets with Daddy. Then this rocket thing comes along. Outer space! Like a Buck Rogers movie, but real. And it's happening right here! Well, part of me wants to just jump into this. But Amy...

RABBI. It's a complicated situation.

AMY. What's so complicated? It seems a matter of morally right and morally wrong. I'd think a Jewish leader would see it that way.

RABBI. Now, you never belonged to a synagogue, you never studied Judaism, so what qualifies you to tell me how a Jewish leader ought to think and behave?

AMY. I'll tell you what I believe. That you're worried what your "non-Jewish friends and neighbors" would say if you spoke out.

JED. Amy, that's too much.

RABBI. I know what happened in Europe as well as you, probably better. I know the millions we lost. Even in our small community we've lost European relatives. I'm a rabbi of a ninety year-old congregation in a small American town. I am not a hunter of war criminals. I have a mission: Replenishment. I have three children and I'm expecting another. It's what I can do. That's my job for the Jewish people. Tell me about yours.

JED. Amy didn't mean any disrespect.

AMY. Jed, don't. *(to RABBI)* I'm thinking about family too. My brother. The children Jed and I would raise here. What would we tell them?

RABBI. I think about that every day. About the children in our religious school. How to tell them what happened in Europe. It's enormous. And it keeps growing. It gets bigger and bigger as we find out more. We don't even have a name for it. It's getting too big to have a name. So how much do we tell the kids? At what age? Do we want them fearing the people in town who have German accents? Scared they'll be coming to hurt them? Yes, I'm thinking of the children. The replenishment of our people, and beyond that, our spirit. Now that's just one big-enough mission for one small town rabbi. So I think I'll just leave the Nazi hunting to the professionals.

AMY. I have my own mission.

RABBI. And you might lose your fight. What will you do if your cause is lost?

AMY. I don't plan on losing.

RABBI. I can see you've got a gift. You're a girl who's got what we call "spark and go." Buckets of it. If you lose, what's gonna happen to all that? You gonna spend your life hurt and angry? Or are you going to put that spark and go to some good use?

(a beat)

JED. And about taking this job?

RABBI. You two are going to be married. You have to start making decisions as a couple. I know, you came for some answers, but rabbis have that way of just asking more questions. *(joking, asking a question)* Isn't that right, Jed?

Scene Five – Israel's Church

(ISRAEL is still at the prayer meetings, wearing his tie, holding his guitar. There's a little sparkle and wink in his "sermon.")

ISRAEL. Here tonight, we're talking about sin. Well, last Saturday night I sinned! Oh, yes, I sinned, and I'll tell y'all just what I did. *(joking with the audience.)* I went out and played gut bucket blues in a low-down juke joint! And I KNOW you good church women think that's a sin! But at this meetin' here in…what we callin' this town now? Rocket City? Here in little ol' Rocket City, Alabam', I'm singin' you my repentance.

ISRAEL. *(Intro)*
I FEEL SO BAD IN THE MORNING
I FEEL SO BAD IN THE MIDDLE OF THE DAY
I FEEL SO BAD IN THE EVENING.
GONNA GO DOWN AND WASH MY SINS AWAY

(Chorus)

GONNA LAY DOWN MY BURDEN
DOWN BY THE RIVERSIDE
DOWN BY THE RIVERSIDE
DOWN BY THE RIVERSIDE
GONNA LAY DOWN MY BURDEN
DOWN BY THE RIVERSIDE
GONNA STUDY WAR NO MORE.

(As the following scenes are played, ISRAEL underscores them with solo guitar music, off of "Down by the Riverside." Lights up on AMY, writing a letter.)

AMY. To the American Jewish Fund. I am writing to inform you of an ongoing situation here in Alabama. I'm sure the many members of the AJF would be outraged to learn that former members of Hitler's war machine are living here and about to become American citizens.

ISRAEL.
GONNA WALK WITH THE PREACHER MAN
DOWN BY THE RIVERSIDE
DOWN BY THE RIVERSIDE…

(Guitar music continues as underscoring. A light comes up on **LESTER** *in* **PIKE***'s office.* **LESTER** *is holding a corked glass bottle with a clear liquid inside.)*

LESTER. Now this ain't any of that Mason jar moonshine, you understand. My boys in the hills, they make some high-quality stuff – what we call 'round here "private label."

*(***LESTER** *hands the bottle to* **MAJOR PIKE***.)*

MAJOR PIKE. Very kind of you, Mr. Pruitt.

LESTER. Call me Lester. Hell, ain't nothin' compared to what you done for me, tippin' me off about the land deals.

MAJOR PIKE. Lester! I told you nothing! And look what you and Mrs. Pruitt have done for me – introducing me to that lovely Miss Louisa Wylie.

LESTER. You could do a lot worse, Major. You know, her grandfather used to be a senator.

MAJOR PIKE. *(of course he knew)* I think she did mention that…

ISRAEL.
DOWN BY THE RIVERSIDE
DOWN BY THE RIVERSIDE…

(Guitar music continues as underscore. Light up on **MRS. DUPRAY***, opening an envelope.)*

MRS. DUPRAY. Now, what's all this with such fancy handwriting? *(reading the return address)* "Von Braun"? I don't know any Von… *(with disdain)* Oh, must be one of those *Germans.*

*(***MRS. DUPRAY** *opens the envelope and reads.)*

MRS. DUPRAY. "My dear Mrs. Dupray. Forgive my intrusion in writing without any introduction to one of the most eminent musical personages in the area. Many of the scientists on my staff…

(Light up on **VON BRAUN***.* **MRS. DUPRAY***'s voice overlaps with* **VON BRAUN***'s as in unison they say the words "Many of the scientists on my staff…")*

VON BRAUN. Many of the scientists on my staff are musicians as well, and they are forming a small concert orchestra. We should be so grateful for your help in selecting pieces that would appeal to our new neighbors in Huntsville. Is it possible you would have the time to share your expertise and serve as our artistic advisor? Very truly yours, *(now accustomed to the Americanized version:)* Dr. Werner Von Brown.

MRS. DUPRAY. *(prayerfully, near tears)* Gracious light of heaven.

*(**MRS. DUPRAY** waves the note towards heaven, bracelets clanking)*

ISRAEL.

GONNA LAY DOWN MY SWORD AND SHIELD
DOWN BY THE RIVERSIDE
GONNA STUDY WAR NO MORE.

(guitar chord button)

Scene Six – Kessler Front Porch

(Lights up on **AMY** *and* **JED** *on the porch.* **JED** *is sitting on the glider.* **AMY** *is reading a letter on a distinctively colored piece of business stationery.)*

AMY. So they got back to me, the Jewish Fund: *(reading letter)* "We have been aware of these Germans since they entered the country. But please understand that we must devote ourselves now to re-uniting and re-settling families from the Nazi era. However, your letter showed a great passion for the Jewish cause and if you are in Washington, please come visit our…" Blah, blah, blah.

JED. As far as they're concerned, the subject is closed.

AMY. Wouldn't you think they'd want to help? Instead, they slam the door. There's no one on my side. Not the government. Not the Jewish groups. Not your rabbi, or anyone else in this town. And maybe not even you, Jed.

JED. Read the letter. They have other priorities. Important ones.

AMY. You know why Pike offered you that job, don't you?

JED. I knew what he was doing. He wanted to get to you. He wants to build his missiles without you getting in the way.

AMY. Do you think I'm wrong?

JED. Listen, I decided I won't take the job if you don't want me to.

AMY. He's just trying to get me to shut up. He just wants…

JED. *(sharply)* What did I just say?

(a beat)

AMY. Well. You've sure learned how to interrupt. *(a beat)* But Jed, you want to work there.

JED. It's exciting. It's getting into outer space on the ground floor, you might say.

AMY. But working beside them?

JED. Like I said, I won't do this if you aren't fine with it.

AMY. And while you're working in the store, you'll hear a rocket take off and you'll think about what you're missing.

JED. I guess I'm not thinkin' that far ahead.

AMY. And what about town fairs and the holiday picnics? Do we make chit-chat with our Nazi neighbors?

JED. I told you what's gonna happen. They'll stay on their side and we'll stay on ours.

AMY. Could we just live somewhere else?

JED. Everything is here. My family. This new opportunity to be part of the future of mankind.

AMY. You sound like Von Braun on the television.

JED. Like I said, it's up to you.

AMY. *(emotion rising)* You SAY that, but it's like you're trying to pressure me in that calm, gentlemanly way.

JED. I'd get through to you if I shouted?

(ISRAEL enters.)

ISRAEL. 'Scuse me. I'm here for Nettie.

JED. Sure, Israel. I think Nettie's upstairs. I'll tell her you're here.

AMY. Jed…

(JED is gone, leaving ISRAEL and AMY alone. A pause.)

ISRAEL. How you enjoying Alabama, Miss Amy?

AMY. Oh, it's a lot different from New York.

(Another pause as ISRAEL decides to pursue a question.)

ISRAEL. Mind if I ask you something – you saying you're from New York City?

AMY. Yes, what'd you want to ask me?

ISRAEL. Do you…you bein' a young woman and all…you ever go much to a baseball game there?

AMY. I used to go with my brother Daniel a lot. He died in the Atlantic during the war.

ISRAEL. I was in the war, too.

AMY. You were?

ISRAEL. France and Italy. Sorry 'bout your brother.

AMY. Thanks. He loved baseball. And I learned to love it so he'd take me to the games.

ISRAEL. And you still go to the games?

AMY. My father and I sometimes go see the Brooklyn Dodgers. Kind of for Daniel. He was a big Dodgers fan, even though we lived in the Bronx where you're supposed to love the Yankees.

ISRAEL. So you seen the Dodgers. You seen Jackie Robinson?

AMY. I have.

ISRAEL. You have. You see, you can't tell from the newsreels. In that Ebbets Field where they play, the white people – they're cheering for him? We was wondering. My friends and me.

AMY. They cheer for him.

ISRAEL. *(skeptical)* Now y'tellin' me the white people in the ballpark are cheerin' for Jackie Robinson?

AMY. Not all. Some don't like it. Don't like him. But most do. Enough to create a big roar.

*(**ISRAEL** is silent as he takes this in. Then he smiles.)*

ISRAEL. *(quietly)* Well, Lord have mercy.

(a beat)

AMY. What branch were you in? Of the military?

ISRAEL. Army.

AMY. Jed was in the Army Air Corps.

ISRAEL. Yes, flyin' his plane, fighting the Nazis. Those Germans in town. I been hearing about what you've been saying. You don't like it.

AMY. No, I don't like it. You've been keeping track of all that?

ISRAEL. Oh, yes I been keeping track. You know I been keeping track. I fought in that war, and I come back here to Nettie and the kids, and I see that these Nazi men, they can go anywhere in town. They can eat in any cafe they want, and us, we can just go to the places we're allowed. Any movie theater, they can sit where they want, and we still got to go up to the balcony, sit upstairs.

(growing increasingly angry and bitter)

Upstairs, in what they call the crow's nest. They can buy a house anywhere in town they want, and we got to...why, I was fighting in Europe while these boys were building bombs for Adolph Hitler! I just didn't think it could get no worse than when I left, but, oh, it got worse, all right, it surely did get worse.

(A pause. AMY gropes for something positive to say.)

AMY. Well – People are cheering in Ebbets Field.

(ISRAEL's mood brightens a bit.)

ISRAEL. And I believe you.

(a beat)

AMY. I tried to do something about the Germans. I don't know what else to do.

ISRAEL. I know what I do.

AMY. What's that?

ISRAEL. I go out and play the blues. I have no idea what y'all do.

(AMY and ISRAEL exchange a smile. JED re-enters.)

JED. Israel, Nettie says to meet her in the garden, she's got some vegetables she's going to bring home. We got a bumper crop of crowder peas.

ISRAEL. So she needs some help with the schleppin'.

JED. Y'might say.

(ISRAEL exits.)

JED. Nothing's changed you know. I still want to spend my life with Amy. I'll sell washing machines, I don't care, I just didn't like what you said, that you're alone with this. You're not alone with this. You want to hand out leaflets or go on strike or send up fireworks, I'm with you. You'd do the same for me. I know you would. Now, put away that letter, it's just upsetting you. Come on, let's tear it up.

AMY. I don't want to tear anything up.

JED. *(sensing her meaning)* I don't either. Why would we?

AMY. Even if you're with me, I know I can't fight this thing. But staying here? Knowing what I know is true, knowing what everyone else is adjusting to or just ignoring. Am I the crazy one?

JED. Not crazy. Maybe if you just give it some time.

AMY. Would you give me that, Jed? Would you give me some time to go off and think about this?

JED. I didn't mean it that way. But if that's what you want, to go off for a while...

*(Lights down. Music transition, **ISRAEL** singing from offstage.)*

ISRAEL.

I'M ALABAMA BOUND
I'M ALABAMA BOUND
AND IF YOU WANT MY LOVIN' BABE
YOU GOT TO LEAVE THIS TOWN

(Music fades out. Sounds of a train idling in the station fade in.)

Scene Seven – Seat on a Northern-Bound Train

(AMY is sitting on a seat in the train, staring out the window. SUSANNA enters.)

SUSANNA. Well, lookit here! My little froggy girl! And heading north this time. *(as she sits)* May I sit with you?

AMY. Oh, yes, please.

(Sound of train leaving station.)

SUSANNA. I'm off to Knoxville again. My weekly visit to Aunt Carol Jean.

AMY. How's she doing?

SUSANNA. Warm weather like this, she says she'll faint dead away if she doesn't get a touch of bourbon. Of course, she says that when it's cold, too.

AMY. Nice of you to take care of her.

SUSANNA. And where are you heading? Up to Chattanooga for a bridal gown fitting?

AMY. Up to New York.

SUSANNA. One look at you, I know it's not the spring fashions bringing you back to New York, is it?

AMY. No, Jed and I are just postponing things for a while.

SUSANNA. I'm so sorry. Case of wedding jitters, am I right? Happens all the time. On my wedding day, my brothers were ready to tie up Lester and haul him to the church like a bale of alfalfa.

AMY. *(smiling a little)* There's a romantic story.

SUSANNA. Oh, Lester didn't know what was best for him. Still doesn't! Now, this "postponement," does it have something to do with your, what do we call it, your little campaign?

AMY. I guess everyone in town knows about that. And hates me.

SUSANNA. I would think Major Pike isn't pleased. When he told us about the Germans moving in, Lester and I weren't too pleased either. But you can't fight city hall, or in this case, the federal government. And believe me, honey, I'm from Alabama. We TRIED.

AMY. I can't figure out how I'm going to live in Huntsville, and ignore those Germans. And Jed…

SUSANNA. …I know, he caught the rocket fever. The whole town has a case of it. So it's back to New York to think things through?

AMY. I guess.

SUSANNA. Well, my mama used to say, if you need to think something through, do it on a train.

AMY. Gets the wheels turning?

SUSANNA. Oh! So that's what she meant! Well, it seems to me the problem is Jed wanting so bad to be in the space program.

AMY. I don't think he'd be happy doing anything else now. And that means staying in Huntsville.

SUSANNA. And where is that written in marble? Not that I'd want to lose you two.

AMY. Where else could we go?

SUSANNA. Well, we'd better think that through, and we'd better do it before we cross the state line. 'Cause Mama used to say, no good thinking ever got done in Tennessee.

(Lights out, train sounds end.)

Scene Eight – Redstone Arsenal

(Stage is dark. **MAJOR PIKE***'s voice is heard in the dark.)*

MAJOR PIKE. I was surprised that you got in touch with me, Amy. I thought we might talk in here this time. Might say I'm feeling like a proud papa, maybe even a show-off. But look, I did it. My promise to the President, I'm delivering it. And I'm delivering it on time.

(Lights up on **AMY** *and* **PIKE***. They are standing at the foot of the Redstone missile as described earlier by* **VON BRAUN***. This is the full-scale version of the miniature model that* **VON BRAUN** *held in his hand when he first entered. The missile is six feet wide. The top of it reaches up, up, up, beyond what's visible on stage.)*

MAJOR PIKE. It's pretty much an adaptation of the V-2. But it's OUR adaptation. Slightly taller, more powerful engine. And what do you think we're calling it, after much consideration, you know what we're naming the baby?

AMY. The Vergeltungswaffe 3.

MAJOR PIKE. Cute. No, we're naming it for this place, for the Redstone Arsenal. Meet the Redstone Missile. And when it's launched, the entire world will know about *(in Southern dialect)* the little ol' Redstone Arsenal in Rocket City, Alabam'.

AMY. So first television, and now you've got another show ready to open. But the script might not go as you've written it.

MAJOR PIKE. Are you still on that? I thought you were coming to me in peace. The Germans are about to be naturalized. Soon you'll be going after American citizens, not foreigners. Can't you just step back and admire what they've done? What they've built here? I mean, just as an object in the world, don't you think it's beautiful? Yes, of course, you can get psychoanalytical about it. But forget that, just think of it as a pure shape, a shape going back to the obelisks of Egypt. Further back! To the prehistoric monoliths still standing in the British Isles.

MAJOR PIKE. *(cont.)* People prayed to those rocket-shaped stones and I bet I know what they were praying for. Protection. And here it is, the answer to an ancient prayer.

The missile is that tall, you know, because most of it is a fuel tank. Everything about it is designed for practicality and physics. A tower of pure function. And yet, look! It turns out to be a thing of beauty.

The most ancient of shapes wedded to the most modern technology. But unlike obelisks and monoliths, THIS BABY CAN FLY! *(to the missile)* CAN'T YOU? YES, FLY! And you'll make the most beautiful of trajectories, the perfect curve of the rainbow, a shape that the Bible tells us was put in the sky by God Himself. Look at this thing, Amy –And you plan to stop it? What do you want to do, kick it? Go ahead. It can take it.

*(**PIKE** kicks the base of the missile.)*

It can take heat up to 2000 degrees Fahrenheit! So why don't we just stand together and admire this supersonic masterpiece that will protect our country and take us through that low-lying sky, past the planets, through the Milky Way, through faraway galaxies, to the entrance of whatever heaven is waiting there beyond.

AMY. *(bluffing)* Your launch will get attention, Major, but it might not be the kind you want.

*(She pulls out the envelope she received from the AJF. She looks **PIKE** straight in the eye, using the slick techniques of truth-bending that she learned from him.)*

You see this envelope? It's from the American Jewish Fund. I can't show you the letter because it contains some details of the rally we're planning on your baby's launch day. Banners. Posters. Swastikas. All that should play well on television. Yeah, I've paid attention to some of your techniques. *(mimicking Pike's delivery and gestures:)* The power of television. So which event will the cameras cover on launching day? That? *(gesturing to the missile)* Or the Nazi exposé?

MAJOR PIKE. *(impressed)* You've gotten to be quite a hard-driving young woman haven't you? Amazing that getting OUT of New York has toughened you up.

AMY. Hard-driving, but with a soft spot. I might be able to persuade them to cancel it.

MAJOR PIKE. You've come to negotiate a truce?

AMY. I have.

MAJOR PIKE. Your terms?

AMY. You talk so much about your personal influence in Washington. I wonder if you're bluffing about that.

MAJOR PIKE. I don't need to bluff.

AMY. You must admit you have a way of adjusting the truth to your purposes.

MAJOR PIKE. Maybe. But not about political influence. I was born into it. And as they say in Washington, influence is affluence.

AMY. You seem very confident about that. Even the Pentagon?

MAJOR PIKE. My speciality.

AMY. *(with an edge)* I believe you know my fiancé Jed? He's working at the family appliance store, but he's looking for a new job.

(A beat as **PIKE** *adds it up.)*

MAJOR PIKE. Ah, I see. Jed at the Pentagon. You two live in Washington, not that far from Jed's family. You get to leave Huntsville and Jed still gets to be in the space program. Clever. So you did find a middle path, not black, not white, but gray. And does Jed know what you're up to?

AMY. That's between Jed and me.

MAJOR PIKE. Good fella that Jed.

AMY. Better than you could possibly imagine.

MAJOR PIKE. And you'd like me to make this happen.

AMY. *(working him)* If you have that kind of influence.

MAJOR PIKE. It'll take one phone call. And then you back off of all this. A deal?

AMY. A deal.

MAJOR PIKE. How do we do this? As two men would?

(He offers his hand.)

AMY. Sure. Let's shake on it.

*(They shake hands. **PIKE** holds on to **AMY**'s hand.)*

MAJOR PIKE. And now, as you once asked me: Was there any truth in what you were telling me? About the rallies, all that?

AMY. Classified information. I know you understand.

*(**AMY** lets go of his hand. **PIKE** smiles.)*

MAJOR PIKE. Well, there's some truth in what I have to say. I believe I'm going to miss you here.

AMY. Oh, Major Pike, you won't be lonely. You have your First Lady in training, Louisa Wylie. And you have your new baby. *(pointing at the Redstone)* I know the three of you will be very happy.

*(Lights out. **ISRAEL**'s solo guitar music, "Down By The Riverside" covers the transition to the final scene.)*

Scene Nine – Countdown, Various Locations

(As music fades out, an offstage voice in the dark intones a classic rocket countdown)

ROCKET VOICE. Fifteen…fourteen…thirteen…twelve…

(Lights come up on **PIKE,** *now* **COLONEL PIKE,** *wearing a uniform reflecting his new rank. He stands face to face with* **VON BRAUN.** *The coldly elegant* **BARONESS VON BRAUN** *stands by her husband, holding his arm.* **SUSANNA** *and* **LESTER** *look on.)*

COLONEL (FORMERLY MAJOR) PIKE. As commanding military officer, I've been allowed by the federal judge present to administer the oath of citizenship. Dr. Von Brown, as leader of the group, you will repeat the words for all assembled. Please raise your right hand.

SUSANNA. Lester, isn't this exiting?

*(***VON BRAUN** *raises his hand.)*

COLONEL PIKE. Repeat after me: "I hereby declare, on oath, that I absolutely and entirely renounce all allegiance and fidelity to any foreign prince, potentate, state or sovereignty of whom or which I have been a subject or citizen."

*(***VON BRAUN** *now speaks in an accented, Americanized English, with well-pronounced W's. He's a relaxed, confident American media figure, ready for the* Time Magazine *cover that's in his future.)*

VON BRAUN. *(solemnly)* I hereby declare, on oath, that I absolutely and entirely renounce all allegiance and fidelity…

(Lights up on a part of the stage where a Jewish wedding is in progress. **JED** *wears a tuxedo and yarmulke.* **AMY** *is in a simple bridal gown.)*

RABBI. Amy, once you were a stranger here, in a strange land. I hope Huntsville has become less of a strange land and more like a second hometown.

ROCKET VOICE. Eleven…ten….nine….

COLONEL PIKE. "That I will support and defend the Constitution and laws of the United States of America against all enemies, foreign and domestic…"

VON BRAUN. That I will support and defend the Constitution and laws of the United States of America…

RABBI. *(to* **JED** *and* **AMY***)* As we greet this new unity called Amy-and-Jed, we must also say farewell. But we feel comforted knowing Amy and Jed will not be all that far away – just up the road a patch, you might say, in Washington D.C. Jed will be working in the Pentagon, as liaison to the Redstone Arsenal Space Program. And we're equally proud that Amy will be going to work in Washington, too, with the American Jewish Fund. She'll be using that wonderful spark and go of hers to re-unite and re-settle families.

ROCKET VOICE. …Eight….seven….six…

COLONEL PIKE. "…without any mental reservation or purpose of evasion, so help me God."

VON BRAUN. …without any mental reservation or purpose of evasion, so help me God.

COLONEL PIKE. Congratulations, citizen.

(**PIKE** *shakes hands with* **VON BRAUN**.)

VON BRAUN. And congratulations to you, *Colonel* Pike. And may I say how pleased I am to be welcome in this country, the beacon of freedom for the entire world.

(**SUSANNA** *takes charge.*)

SUSANNA. Hello, y'all. I'm just so happy to be the lucky lady chosen to declare this "New Citizens Day!" On a personal note, I'd like to congratulate all of these new Americans, especially Baron von Brown. And you, too, Baroness, my new pal. We sure had a ball at that fish fry, didn't we, honey?

(*The* **BARONESS**, *with the memory of the fried food still too vivid, gives* **SUSANNA** *a chilly smile and nod.* **SUSANNA** *chooses to react as if she'd just been thrown a big kiss.*)

SUSANNA. She is a DEAR!

ROCKET VOICE. …five….four…

RABBI. At the breaking of the wine glass, many non-Jews wonder what this ritual means. Many Jews wonder, too. And you'll hear as many explanations as there are rabbis. But there is one that I especially embrace. On this happiest of occasions, we remember that there is still heartbreak in the world. A gloomy thought! Sadness on this day of joy! But the ritual also reminds us of the opposite – that in the darkest of times, and those times come, there will always be a small spark of joy and eventually, a replenishment of the light. Jed, you will please break the glass.

ROCKET VOICE. …three….two….one…

*(At the moment **JED** stomps on the glass there is a sound effect of a: HUGE BOOM! – the same sound that opened the play. The **ROCKET VOICE** continues over the reverberating thunder of the rocket launch.)*

ROCKET VOICE. And we have lift-off! The Redstone, the first American guided missile, has left the launching pad here in Cape Canaveral, Florida.

*(**JED** and **AMY** kiss. Guitar music, instrumental of "Down By The Riverside" sneaks in.)*

ROCKET VOICE. It's a day for the history books, one to remember always! The day our country enters the Space Age!

*(All turn and gaze at the missile on stage. **ISRAEL** sings and plays guitar over the fading sound of the blast. He sings the last three lines of "Down By The Riverside.")*

ISRAEL.
…DOWN BY THE RIVERSIDE
GONNA STUDY WAR NO MORE
WE AIN'T GONNA STUDY WAR…

(Singing and guitar music out.)

ISRAEL. *(speaking firmly, quietly)* No more.

(Lights out on everything except the Redstone Missile. The light on the missile remains for a few beats. Then blackout.)

The End

COSTUME PLOT

AMY LUBIN
    Smart traveling clothes including hat and gloves
    Skirt
    Top
    Overcoat
    Hat
    Jacket
    Simple bridal gown

MAJOR HAMILTON PIKE JR.
    Military pinks
    Civilian clothes
    Military uniform with Colonel rankings

JED KESSLER
    Casual wear
    Jacket
    Pants
    Tuxedo

WERNHER VON BRAUN
    Well-tailored suit

ISRAEL WATKINS
    Work clothes
    Dark suit
    Open-collar white shirt
    Tie

Character Man 1: **HARRY S. TRUMAN, BENJY, LEMUEL DECATUR, LESTER PRUITT, ROCKET VOICE**
    Suit
    Bowtie, wire-rim glasses (Truman)
    Working-class London casuals (Benjy)

Character Man 2: **GENERAL BARKLEE, HEINZ KLAUBER, RABBI BENJAMIN, ANNOUNCER**
    Military uniform (General Barklee)
    Casuals, but European and out-of-place (Klauber)
    Casuals (Rabbi)

Character Woman 1: **SUSANNA PRUITT, SARAH OF LONDON**
    Stylish traveling outfit with banjo-shaped brooch (Susanna)
    Various fashionable dresses

Character Woman 2: **BERTINA DUPRAY, EUVELLA, POLLY, BARONESS VON BRAUN**
    Dress
    Charm bracelets (Dupray)
    Work apron (Euvella)
    Rocket hat (Euvella)
    British military uniform (Polly)
    Severe, stylish dress (Baroness)

PROPERTIES LIST

Act 1 – Scene 1
   N/A

Act 1 – Scene 2
   Map (must roll up)
   A document
   Pen
   Musical instruments: solo guitar.

Act 1 – Scene 3
   Newspaper clippings
   Compact mirror
   Makeup bag
   Makeup
   Engagement ring
   Travel cases

Act 1 – Scene 4
   Map
   Document
   Pen
   Small American flag
   Small Confederate flag

Act 1 – Scene 5
   Hanky

Act 1 – Scene 6
   Pad
   Pencil
   Purse

Act 1 – Scene 7
   Bottle of spray ammonia
   Mop
   Package of rubber gloves
   Cleaning fluid
   Can of household cleaning oil
   Cash
   Coins

Act 1 – Scene 8
   Model of Redstone missile
   Von Braun file

Act 1 – Scene 9
    Oil
    Cleaning cloth
    Letter on stationery (Amy's copy)
    Letter on stationery (Susanna's copy)

Act 1 – Scene 10
    Letter on stationery (Pike's copy)
    Amy Lupin file
    Purse

Act 1 – Scene 11
    Picnic basket
    Spray bottle of ammonia
    Jar of sauerkraut
    String of bratwurst
    Bottle of Riesling wine
    Cloth
    Rubber gloves
    Pink envelope

Act 1 – Scene 12
    Library book
    Paper with job description and salary written on it

Act 2 – Scene 1
    Large model of Redstone missile with small panel on its side that opens
    Plate of cookies
    Cocktail

Act 2 – Scene 2
     Leaflet
    United States map
    Elevation (diagram) of rocket
    Clutch purse

Act 2 – Scene 3
    Pink stationery
    Pen
    Promotional potholders

Act 2 – Scene 4
    N/A

Act 2 – Scene 5
    Letter on stationery
    "Private label" clear alcohol bottle
    Letter in envelope

Act 2 – Scene 6
    Large glass
    Letter and envelope

Act 2 – Scene 7
    Travel cases

Act 2 – Scene 8
    Purse
    Envelope with letter inside

Act 2 – Scene 9
    Purse
    Prayer book
    Wine glass wrapped in white cloth (a light bulb can be used in place of wine glass.)

SET NOTES

We approached the design of *ROCKET CITY, ALABAM'* deciding the star of the show is the Redstone Missile which is being constructed throughout the play. So in the set design, the Big Entrance of the Star needs to be considered at the outset. The missile itself is really just a tall cylinder, painted to be a Redstone. The challenge of stashing it away until its entrance was solved ingeniously in the Alabama Shakespeare Festival production. The Redstone was hidden behind curved doors that were on tracks. It sat there behind those upstage doors for the bulk of the play. Then, during a blackout, the doors were parted and when the lights came up, the missile was magically present.

The rest of the set was conceived around several levels, which were freely used to represent the various locations in the town adding a minimum of set pieces. This enabled a smooth and constant flow of the play, which is essential. The stage at ASF was 3/4 round, and a proscenium stage would no doubt present some other creative design solutions, but the presence and reveal of the Redstone should be considered first off.

FLOOR PLAN
"Rocket City, Alabam'"
Octagon Theatre, Alabama Shakespeare Festival

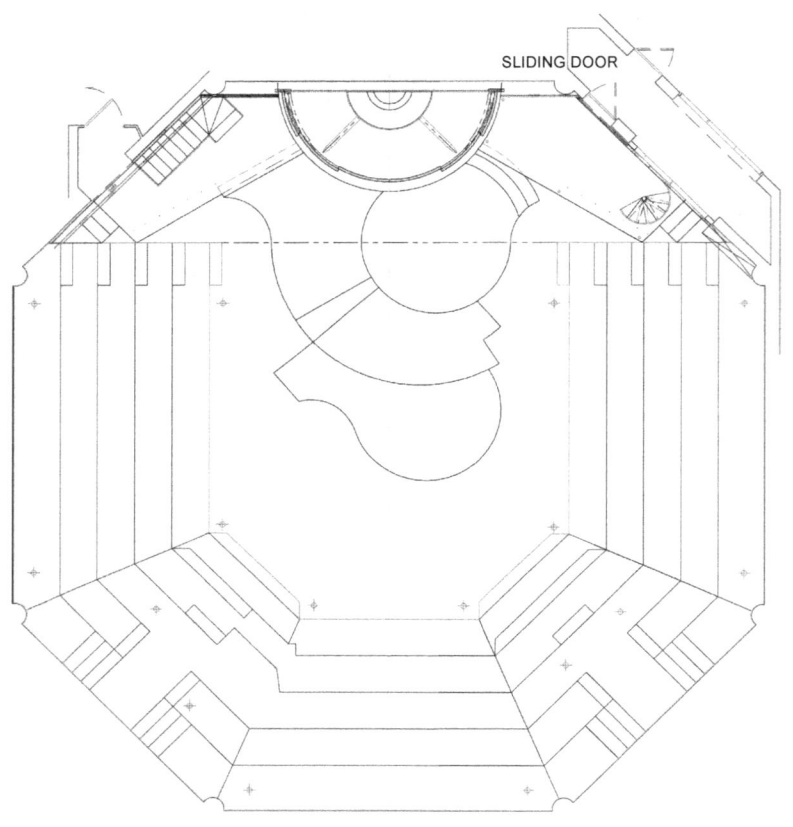

SLIDING DOOR

OTHER TITLES AVAILABLE FROM SAMUEL FRENCH

A...MY NAME IS ALICE

Joan Micklin Silver and Julianne Boyd

Musical Revue / 5f / Bare stage w. set pieces.

Originally produced by the Women's Project at the American Place Theatre in New York, Alice enjoyed a long run at the Village Gate Off Broadway. This slick and lively revue created by a wide variety of comedy writers, lyricists and composers offers a marvelous kaleidoscope of contemporary women. Sophisticated, bawdy, funny and insightful, the twenty numbers portray friends, rivals, sisters and even members of an all women's basketball team. Winner of the Outer Critics' Circle Award, Best Musical.

"Delightful...The music and lyrics are so sophisticated that they can carry the weight of one act plays."
– *The New York Times*

"A boodle of laughs."
– *New York Post*

"Rates an A!."
– *New York Daily News*

"Slick as can be."
– *Village Voice*